THE MOTION PICTU
CHUMS AT SEASIDE PARK

BY

VICTOR APPLETON

THE MOTION PICTURE CHUMS AT SEASIDE PARK

CHAPTER I—LOOKING FOR BUSINESS

"Boys, this is just the spot we are looking for!"

"Yes, I am sure a good photo playhouse on this boardwalk would pay."

It was Frank Durham who made the first declaration and his chum and young partner, Randy Powell, who echoed it. Both looked like lads in business earnestly looking for something they wanted, and determined to find it. Then the third member of the little group glanced where his companions were gazing. He was Pepperill Smith, and he burst forth in his enthusiastic way:

"The very thing!"

The three chums had arrived at Seaside Park only that morning. Their home was at Fairlands, one hundred and fifty miles west. Everything was new to them and there was certainly enough variety, excitement and commotion to satisfy any lively lad. They had, however, come for something else than pleasure. They had a distinct purpose in view, and Frank's remarks brought it up.

Seaside Park was a very popular ocean resort. It was a trim little town with a normal population of less than three thousand souls. In the summer season, however, it provided for over ten times that number. A substantial boardwalk fronted the beach where people bathed, lined with stores, booths, and curio and souvenir tents. There were several restaurants for the convenience of those who had run down from the big cities to take a day's enjoyment and did not care to stay at the pretentious hotels.

The three friends had made for this part of the resort as soon as they had arrived. As they had strolled down the boardwalk Frank had studiously observed the general layout and the points where the pleasure-seekers most congregated. Randy was quite as much interested in peering in at the windows of the few buildings bearing "To Rent" signs. Pep made a deliberate stop wherever a show place attracted his attention. Now all three had halted in front of an unoccupied building and were looking it over critically.

"I say, fellows," observed Frank, "this is worth looking into."

"It's certainly a fine location," added Randy.

"Just made for us," piped the exuberant Pep.

The building was frame and one story in height. It was of ample breadth, and as the brisk and busy Pep squinted down its side he declared it was over one hundred feet long. Randy went up to the chalked-over windows, while Frank took out a card and copied the name and address of the owner given on the rent sign.

"Hi, this way!" suddenly hailed the active Pep. "The door isn't locked."

"That's great," spoke Randy. "I want to see what the inside looks like."

"Hello, there!" called out a man's voice as they stepped over the threshold of the broad double doorway.

"Hello yourself, mister," retorted Pep cheerily, "we were sort of interested in the place and wanted to look it over."

Frank stepped forward. The man who had challenged them was in his shirt sleeves, working at a plank over two wooden horses mending some wire screens.

"We are looking over the beach with the idea of finding a good location for a show," Frank explained.

"What kind of a show?" inquired the man, studying the trio sharply.

"Motion picture."

"Well, you've come to the right place, I can tell you that," declared the man, showing more interest and putting aside the screen he was mending. "Pretty young, though, for business on your own hook; aren't you?"

"Oh, we're regular business men, we are," vaunted Pep. "This is Frank Durham, and this is Randolph Powell. The three of us ran a photo playhouse in Fairlands for six months, so we know the business."

"Is that so?" observed the man musingly. "Well, I'm the owner of the building here and as you see, want to find a good tenant for the season. I'm mending up the screens to those ventilating windows. I'm going to redecorate it inside and out, and the place is right in the center of the busiest part of the beach."

"What was it used for before?" inquired Frank.

"Bowling alley, once. Then a man tried an ice cream parlor, but there was too much competition. Last season a man put in a penny arcade, but that caught only the cheap trade and not much of that."

Frank walked to the end of the long room and looked over the lighting equipment, the floor and the ceiling. Then he nodded to Randy and Pep, who joined him at a window, as if looking casually over the surroundings of the vacant place.

"See here, fellows," Frank said, "it looks as though we had stumbled upon a fine opportunity."

"Splendid!" voiced Randy.

"It strikes me just right," approved Pep. "What a dandy place we can make of it, with all this space! Why, we'll put three rows of seats, the middle one double. There's all kinds of space on the walls for posters. I'll have to get an assistant usher and——"

"Hold on, Pep!" laughed Frank. "Aren't you going pretty fast? The rent may be 'way out of our reach. You know we are not exactly millionaires, and our limited capital may not come anywhere near covering things."

"Find out what the rent is; won't you, Frank?" pressed Randy.

"There's no harm in that," replied Frank.

He went up to the owner of the place while Randy and Pep strolled outside. They walked around the building twice, studying it in every particular. Randy looked eager and Pep excited as Frank came out on the sidewalk. They could tell from the pleased look on his face that he was the bearer of good news.

"What is it, Frank?" queried Randy, anxiously.

"The rent isn't half what I expected it to be."

"Good!" cried Pep.

"But it's high enough to consider in a careful way. Then again the owner of the building insists that nothing but a strictly first-class show will draw patronage at Seaside Park. The people who come here are generally of a superior type and the transients come from large places where they have seen the best going in the way of photo plays. It's going to cost a lot of money to start a playhouse here, and we can't decide in a moment."

"How many other motion picture shows are there in Seaside Park, Frank?" inquired Pep.

"None."

Both Randy and Pep were surprised at this statement and told Frank so.

"The movies tried it out in connection with a restaurant last season, but made a fizzle of it, the man in there tells me," reported Frank. "He says there may be a show put in later in the season—you see we are pretty early on the scene and the summer rush has not come yet. In fact, he hinted that some New York fellows were down here last week looking over the prospects in our line. I've told him just how we are situated, and I think he has taken quite a liking to us and would like to encourage us if it didn't cost him anything. He says he will give us until Monday to figure up and decide what we want to do. There's one thing, though—we will have to put up the rent for the place for the whole season."

"What—in advance?" exclaimed Randy.

"Yes—four months. It seems that one or two former tenants left their landlord in the lurch and he won't take any more risks. Cash or the guarantee of some responsible person is the way this man, Mr. Morton, puts in."

"Humph!" commented Pep. "Why doesn't he make us buy the place and be done with it?"

"Well, if we start in we're going to stick; aren't we?" propounded Randy. "So it's simply a question of raising enough money."

"Mr. Morton says that along Beach Row there is nothing in the way of first-class amusements," Frank went on. "There's a merry-go-round and a summer garden with a band and some few cheap side shows."

"Then we would have the field all to ourselves," submitted Randy.

"Unless a business rival came along, which he won't, unless we are making money, so the more the merrier," declared Frank, briskly. "We'll talk the whole business over this evening, fellows. In the meantime we'll take in the many sights and post ourselves on the prospects."

"I do hope we'll be able to get that place," said Pep, longingly. "What a fine view we have! I'd never get tired of being in sight of the sea and all this gay excitement around us."

The chums left the boardwalk and went across the sands, watching the merry crowds playing on the beach and running out into the water. Big and little, old and young, seemed to be full of fun and excitement. Early in the season as it was, there were a number of bathers.

"That would make a fine motion picture; eh?" suggested Randy, his mind always on business.

"Yes, and so would that!" shouted Pep. "Jumping crickets! Fellows—look!"

There had sounded a sharp explosion. At a certain spot a great cascade of water like the spouting of a whale went up into the air. A hiss of steam focussed in a whirling, swaying mass at one point. There was the echo of yells and screams.

"What's happened, I wonder——" began Randy.

"I saw it!" interrupted an excited bather, who had ran out of the water. "A motor boat has blown up!"

"Then those on board must be in danger of burning or drowning, boys," shouted Frank. "To the rescue!"

CHAPTER II—THE MOTOR BOAT

Frank Durham was just as practical as he was heroic. While the frightened people in the water were rushing up the beach in a panic, and strollers along the sands stared helplessly toward the scene of the accident, Frank's quick eye took in the situation—and in a flash he acted.

There was a reason why he was so ready-witted. In the first place he—and also Randy and Pep—had for an entire season been in actual service at the outing resort near their home town of Fairlands. It had been an experience that fitted them for just such a crisis as the present one. Boating on the lake had been the principal diversion of the guests. There had been more than one tip-over in which Frank and his chums had come to the rescue.

In fact, while the boys had regular duties, such as acting as caddies for golfers, as guides and chauffeurs, the proprietor of the resort expected them to keep an eye out at all times for mishaps to his guests. This had trained the chums in a line where common sense, speedy action, and knowing how to do just the right thing at just the right time, would be useful in safe-guarding property and human life.

Frank did not have to tell his companions what to do. They knew their duty and how far they could be useful, as well as their leader. The motor boat was about a quarter of a mile out and was on fire. They could see the flames belching out at the stern. There seemed to be three or four persons aboard. As far as they could make it out at the distance they were, one of the passengers had sprung overboard and was floating around on a box or plank. The others were crowded together at the bow, trying to keep away from the flames.

Randy had dashed down the beach to where there was a light rowboat overturned on the sand. Pep was making for a long pier running out quite a distance, pulling off his coat as he went. Frank had his eyes fixed upon a small electric launch lying near the pier. He did not know nor notice what course his chums had taken. He realized that if help came to the people in peril on the motor boat it must come speedily to be of any avail.

It took Frank less than three minutes to reach the spot where a light cable held the launch against the pier. A rather fine-looking old man stood nearby, glancing through his gold-rimmed eyeglasses toward the beach, as if impatient of something.

"Mister," shot out Frank, breathlessly, "is this your craft?"

"It is," replied the gentleman. "I am waiting for my man to come and run me down to Rock Point."

"Did you see that?" inquired Frank, rapidly, pointing to the burning motor boat.

"Why, I declare—I hadn't!" exclaimed the man, taking a survey of the point in the distance indicated by Frank. "What can have happened?"

"An explosion, sir," explained Frank. "You see, they must have help."

"Where is that laggard man of mine?" cried the owner of the launch, growing excited. "If he would come we might do something."

"Let me take your launch," pressed Frank, eagerly.

"Do you know how to run it?"

"Oh, yes, sir."

"I don't. Do your best, lad. You must hurry. The boat is burning fiercely."

It only needed the word of assent to start Frank on his mission of rescue. There had never been a better engineer on the lake near Fairlands than our hero. He was so perfectly at home with a launch that the owner of the one he had immediately sprung into could not repress a "Bravo!" as Frank seemed to slip the painter, spring to the wheel and send the craft plowing the water like a fish, all with one and the same deft movement.

Frank estimated time and distance and set the launch on a swift, diagonal course. He made out a rowboat headed in the same direction as himself, and Randy was in it. Frank saw a flying form leave the end of the long pier in a bold dive. It was Pep. Frank could not deviate or linger, for the nearer he got to the blazing craft the more vital seemed the peril of those now nearly crowded overboard by the heat and smoke. Besides that, he knew perfectly well that the crack swimmer of Fairlands, his friend Pep, could take care of himself in the water.

It was because the three chums were always together and always on the alert that nothing missed them. Some pretty creditable things had been done by them and that training came to their help in the present crisis.

In the first volume of the present series, entitled "The Motion Picture Chums' First Venture; Or, Opening a Photo Playhouse in Fairlands," their adventures and experiences have been given in a way that showed the courage and enterprise that infused them. Frank Durham was the elder of the trio, and it was he who had started a partnership that soon outgrew odd chores about Fairlands and making themselves handy around the lake during the outing season.

Early in the Fall preceding, after a great deal of thinking, planning and actual hard work, Frank, Randy and Pep had become proprietors of a motion picture show at Fairlands. It had been no play-day spurt, but a practical business effort. They had worked hard for nearly a year, had saved up quite a sum, and learning of the auction sale of a photo playhouse outfit in the city, they had bid it in and started the "Wonderland" in the busy little town where they lived.

In this they had been greatly helped by a good-hearted, impulsive fellow named Ben Jolly. The latter was in love with the novel enterprise, liked the boys, and played the piano. Another of his kind who was a professional ventriloquist, had plied his art for the benefit of the motion picture show, delaying the auction sale with mock bids until Frank arrived in time to buy the city outfit.

They had enemies, too, and the son of a Fairlands magnate named Greg Grayson had caused them a good deal of trouble and had tried to break up their show. Perseverance, hard work and brains, however, carried the motion picture chums through. They exhibited none but high-grade films, they ran an orderly place, and with Frank at the projector, Randy in the ticket booth, Pep as the genial usher and Ben Jolly as pianist, they had crowded houses and wound up at the end of the season out of debt and with a small cash capital all their own.

For all the busy Winter, warm weather hurt the photo playhouse at Fairlands. It had been a debated question with the chums for some weeks as to shutting down for the summer months. They finally decided to "close for repairs" for a spell and look around for a new location until fall. Seaside Park was suggested as an ideal place for a first-class motion picture show, and so far prospects looked very encouraging, indeed.

Right in the midst of their business deliberations the incident just related had now come up. All three of the boys had answered the call of humanity without an instant's hesitation.

Frank forgot everything except the business in hand as he set eyes, mind and nerve upon reaching the burning motor boat in time to be of some practical service. He was near enough now to pretty well grasp the situation. The launch had been going at a high rate of speed, but the expert young engineer set the lever another notch forward, and sent the craft slipping through the water like a dolphin.

The man in charge of the burning boat, Frank saw, had a pan with a handle. He was dipping this into the water and throwing its contents against the blazing after-part of the boat. Some gasoline or other inflammable substance, however, seemed to burn all the more fiercely for this deluge, and the man had to shrink farther and farther away as the flames encroached upon him.

A portly lady was shrieking constantly and waving her arms in a state of terror. It was all that a younger woman, the other passenger, could do to hold her in her seat and restrain her from jumping overboard.

Frank had just a passing glance for the other actor in the scene. This was the fellow he had seen leap overboard when the boat blew up. He was somewhat older than Frank, and having cast adrift a box, the only loose article aboard that would serve to act as a float, he had drifted safely out of reach of the flames.

"He's a coward, besides being a cad," involuntarily flashed through Frank's mind. Then he made the launch swerve, and shouted to the occupants of the motor boat:

"All ready!"

Frank, with his experience of the past, calculated so nicely that the launch came alongside the burning motor boat at precisely the right angle to allow the man in charge of the latter craft to grapple with a boat-hook.

"Quick, Mrs. Carrington," he spoke to the older lady, "get aboard the launch as fast as you can."

The woman's girl companion helped her get to her feet, but she pitched about so that but for a clever movement on the part of Frank she would have gone into the water.

"Oh, dear! oh, dear!" she screamed, but with the aid of the younger woman Frank managed to get her into the launch, where she dropped in a heap and went into hysterics. Her companion got aboard more quietly.

"You are just in time," gasped the man in charge of the motor boat. "Don't risk the flames, but pull away."

"Yes, there is nothing to be done in the way of putting out the fire," said Frank.

The man he spoke to was both worried and in pain. His face and hands were blistered from his efforts to shield his passengers from the fire. Just then a howl rang out. It proceeded from the fellow thirty feet away, bobbing up and down on the empty box. This brought the older woman to her senses.

"It is Peter!" she screamed. "Oh, save Peter!"

The paltry Peter began bellowing with deadly fear as the launch was headed away from him. Frank could not feel very charitable toward a fellow who, in the midst of peril, had left friends, probably relatives, to their fate. However, he started to change the course of the launch, when Pep, swinging one arm over the other in masterly progress like the fine swimmer he always had been, crossed the bow of the craft.

"I'll take care of him," shouted Pep to Frank, "and here's Randy in the skiff."

Frank saw Randy making for the spot, and as Pep grasped the side of the floating box the skiff came alongside.

"Hold on! Stop that other boat," blubbered the young fellow. "I want to go ashore in a safe rig; I want to get to my aunt."

"What did you leave her for?" demanded Pep, firing up.

"Huh! Think I want to get drowned?" whimpered the other.

Pep helped the scared youth into the skiff, drew himself over its edge, and directed just one remark to the rescued lad.

"Say!" he observed, indignantly. "I'd just like to kick you."

CHAPTER III—SHORT OF FUNDS

Frank drove the motor launch shoreward with accuracy and speed. The stout lady had shrieked and acted as if half mad until she had been assured that Peter was safe. She had to see with her own eyes that Peter had been pulled into the rowboat with Randy and Pep. Then she collapsed again.

While she lay limp and exhausted, the young lady with her mopped her head with a handkerchief and fanned her. The engineer of the motor boat had got near to Frank. He looked pale and distressed. He kept his eye fixed on the sinking motor boat for a time.

"That's the last of her," he remarked, with a sigh.

"Yes," responded Frank, "we couldn't do anything toward saving her."

"I should think not. I tell you, if you hadn't known your business I don't know what would have happened to us. Mrs. Carrington was entirely unmanageable, her companion can't swim, and of course I wouldn't leave them to perish."

"The stout lady is Mrs. Carrington, I suppose?" asked Frank.

"That's right."

"And Peter, I suppose, is the brave young man who jumped overboard with the float?"

"He is her nephew, and a precious kind of a relative he is!" said the motor boat man, and his face expressed anger and disgust. "He would smoke those nasty cigarettes of his and throw the stubs where he liked. Honestly, I believe it was one of those that started the fire."

"He hasn't shown himself to be very valiant or courageous," commented Frank.

There was a great crowd at the beach near the shore end of the pier where the launch landed. The skiff holding Randy, Pep and their dripping and shivering companion glided to the same spot as an officer saw that the launch was secured. He stared down in an undecided way at the helpless Mrs. Carrington. Peter, safe and sound now, leaped aboard the launch with the assurance of an admiral.

"Hey, officer," he hailed the man, "get a conveyance for the party as quick as you can."

"Suppose you do it yourself?" growled the motor boat man, looking as if he would like to give Peter a good thrashing.

"Me? In this rig? Oh, dear, no!" retorted the shocked Peter. "I've got five suits of clothes home. Really, I ought to send for one. Don't know what the people at Catalpa Terrace will say to see me coming home looking like a drowned rat, don't you know," and Peter grinned in a silly, self-important way.

"He makes me sick!" blurted out the motor boat man.

The young lady who was supporting Mrs. Carrington leaned toward Frank. Her face expressed the respect and admiration she felt for their rescuer.

"We can never thank you enough for your prompt service," she said, in a voice that trembled a trifle from excitement.

"I am glad I was within call," replied Frank, modestly.

"Won't you kindly give me your name?" inquired the young lady. "I am Miss Porter, and I am companion to Mrs. Carrington. I know her ways so well, that I am sure the first thing she will want to know when she becomes herself again is the name of her brave rescuer."

"My name is Frank Durham," replied our hero. "My chums in the little boat are Randolph Powell and Pepperill Smith."

"So you live here at Seaside Park? Where can Mrs. Carrington send you word, for I am positive she will wish to see you?"

"We may stay here until to-morrow—I cannot tell," explained Frank. "If we do, I think we will be at the Beach Hotel."

The young lady had a small writing tablet with a tiny pencil attached, secured by a ribbon at her waist. She made some notations. Then she extended her hand and grasped Frank's with the fervency of a grateful and appreciative person. Then an auto cab drew up at the end of the pier, the officer summoned help, and Mrs. Carrington was lifted from the launch. Frank assisted Miss Porter, and Peter, apparently fancying himself an object of admiration to all the focussed eyes of the crowd, disappeared into the automobile.

"Hey!" yelled Pep after him, doubling his fists. "Thank you!"

The motor boat man grasped Frank's hand with honest thankfulness in his eyes.

"I shan't forget you very soon," he said with genuine feeling.

"Did the boat belong to you?" asked Frank.

"Yes, I own two motor boats here," explained the man, "and run them for just such parties as you see."

"The explosion will cause you some money loss."

"I hardly think so," answered the man. "Mrs. Carrington is a rich woman, they say, and she is quite liberal, too. I think she will do the right thing and not leave all the loss on a poor man like myself."

"Get the skiff back where you found it, Randy," directed Frank. "I will be with you soon," and he started the launch back for the spot where he had been allowed to use it by its owner.

A chorus of cheers followed him. Glancing across the pier, Frank noted the owner of the motor boat surrounded by a crowd and being interviewed by two young fellows who looked like newspaper reporters. One of them parted the throng suddenly and ran along the pier, focussing a camera upon the launch. He took a snap shot and waved his hand with an admiring gesture at its operator.

"Young man, I don't know when I have been so pleased and proud," observed the owner of the launch as Frank drove up to the pier where he stood. "I'm glad I had my boat at hand and as bright and smart a fellow as you to run it just in the nick of time."

Frank felt pleased over his efforts to be helpful to others. He was too boyish and ingenuous not to suffer some embarrassment as he passed little groups staring after him. Such remarks as "That's him!" "There he goes!" "Plucky fellow!" and the like greeted his hearing and made him blush consciously.

He found his friends down the beach, Randy laughing at Pep and joking with him, the latter seated on the edge of the boardwalk emptying the water out of his shoes and grumbling at a great rate.

"What's the trouble, Pep?" hailed Frank.

"Trouble! Say, whenever I think of my chance to duck that cheap cad we took aboard the skiff I want to lam myself. 'Jumped overboard to hurry for help,' he claimed. Then found 'that he had forgotten he couldn't swim.' Bah!" and the irate Pep slammed his shoe down on a board as if it was the head of the offensive and offending Peter Carrington.

"We'll go up town and get you dried out, Pep," remarked Frank. "I say, fellows, I'm inclined to believe that we're going to find an opportunity of some kind here at Seaside Park. The little hotel we inquired at seems to be the cheapest in the place, and we had better make arrangements there for a sort of headquarters, even if we don't stay here more than a day or two."

"That suits," nodded Randy. "The man offered a double room on the top floor for a dollar, and we can pick up our meals outside."

The three chums concluded the arrangement at the Beach Hotel. Fortunately each had brought an extra suit of clothes on his journey, and Pep was placed in comfortable trim once more. Then they sallied forth again to make a tour of the parts of the little town they had not previously visited.

"Just look at the crowds right within a stone's throw of the place we are thinking of renting," said Pep, as quite naturally they wandered back to the empty store so suited to their purposes and so desired by each.

"Yes, and it keeps up from almost daybreak clear up to midnight," declared Randy. "Why, Frank, we could run three shifts four hours each. Just think of it—twelve shows a day. Say, it would be a gold mine!"

"I agree with you that it looks very promising," decided Frank. "We must do some close figuring, fellows."

"Let's go inside and look the building over again," suggested Pep, and this they did.

"Why, hello!" instantly exclaimed the owner. "Back again?"

"Yes, Mr. Morton," replied Frank, pleasantly.

"Shake!" cried the old fellow, dropping a hammer he held and in turn grasping a hand of each of his juvenile visitors. "You're some pluck, the three of you. That was the neatest round-up I ever saw. What you been before? Life saving service?"

"Why, hardly——" began Frank.

"Well, you got those people off that burning motor boat slicker than I ever saw it done before. Look here, lads, business is business, and I have to hustle too hard for the dollars to take any risks, but I like the way you do things, and if I can help you figure out how you may take a lease on the premises here and make something out of the old barracks, I'm going to favor you."

"We shall decide this evening, Mr. Morton," said Frank.

"Well, you've got an option on the place till you are ready to report, no matter who comes along."

"Thank you," bowed Frank.

"Oh, I do so hope we can make it!" exclaimed the impetuous Pep.

They were hungry enough to enjoy a hearty meal at a restaurant. Then they found themselves tired enough for a resting spell. Their room at the hotel was a lofty one, but it commanded the whole beach and afforded an unobstructed view of the sea for miles. The chums arranged their chairs so as to catch the cool breeze coming off the water, forming a half-circle about an open window.

Frank had been pretty quiet since they had last seen the vacant store, leaving Randy and Pep to do the chattering. They knew their business chum had been doing some close calculating and they eagerly awaited his first word.

"Tell you, fellows," finally spoke their leader in an offhand but serious way, "I've turned and twisted about all the many corners to this big proposition before us, and it's no trivial responsibility for amateurs like us."

"We made good at Fairlands; didn't we?" challenged Pep.

"That is true," admitted Frank, "but remember our investment there wasn't heavy; we didn't have to go into debt, expenses were light, we were right among friends who wanted to encourage us, and we had free board at home."

"That's so," murmured Randy, with a long-drawn sigh.

"If we start in here at Seaside Park," went on Frank, "we have got to fix up right up to date or we'll find ourselves nowhere in a very little while. There's electric fans, expensive advertising, a big license fee, more help and the films—that's the feature that worries me. As we learned this morning, we have got to have the latest and best in that direction."

"But twelve shows a day, Frank," urged Pep. "Think of it—twelve!"

"Yes, I know," responded Frank. "It looks very easy until some break comes along. I wouldn't like to pile up a lot of expenses, and then have to flunk and lose not only the little capital we have but the outfit we've worked so hard to get. Truth is, fellows, any way I figure it out, we're short of the ready funds to carry this thing through."

Randy and Pep looked pretty blank at this. It was a decidedly wet blanket on all their high hopes.

"Couldn't we get a partner who would finance us?" finally suggested Randy.

"Why, say, give me that chance!" spoke an eager voice that brought the three chums to their feet.

CHAPTER IV—AN OLD FRIEND

It had grown nearly dusk while the three chums sat at the window of their room animatedly discussing their prospects. None of them had thought of lighting the gas and the night shadows that had crept into the room prevented them from recognizing the intruder whom they now faced.

They had left the door of the room leading into the corridor wide open to allow a free current of air. The doorway framed a dim figure who now advanced into the room as Frank challenged sharply:

"Who's that?"

"Why, it's me—Peter," came the cool reply. "Don't you remember?"

Peter—Peter Carrington—stalked closer to the window with the superb effrontery that was a natural part of his make-up. He ducked his head and grinned at the chums in the most familiar manner in the world. There was a spare chair near by. Peter moved it near to the others and sat down as if he owned it.

"Feels good to rest," he enlightened his grim and astonished hosts. "Had a message for you, and the hotel clerk directed me to your room. Say, you must fancy climbing four flights of stairs!"

"You seem to have made it," observed Randy, in a rather hostile tone, while Pep seemed bristling all over.

"Glad I did," piped Peter, cheerfully. "Wouldn't have missed it for worlds. Just in time to hear you fellows going over your dandy scheme, and say—it's a winner! Photo playhouse on the beach! Why, it'll coin money!"

Nobody said anything. Frank was minded to treat the intruder civilly and resumed his chair. Suddenly Pep flared out:

"Have you been waiting out in the hall there, listening to our private conversation?"

"Guess I have; glad I did," chuckled the thick-skinned Peter. "I heard you say you were short of funds and something about a partner. What's the matter with me? I suppose you know my aunt is rich and we're some folks here. We live up on the Terrace—most fashionable part of the town. Why, if I had an interest in your show I could fill your place with complimentaries to the real people of Seaside Park. They'd advertise you, my friends would, till there'd be nothing but standing room left."

"Think so?" observed Randy, drily.

"Know it. I'm my aunt's heir, you know, and she's got scads of money. She's been drawing the tight rein on me lately. I smashed an automobile last week and it cost her over four hundred dollars, and she's holding me pretty close on the money question. But in business, she'd stake me for anything I wanted. Says she wants to see me get into something."

"You got into the water when the motor boat blew up, all right," remarked Pep.

"Hey?" spoke Peter, struggling over the suggestion presented. "Oh, you mean a joke? Ha! ha! yes, indeed. Business, though, now," and Peter tried to look shrewd and important.

"We have not yet decided what we are going to do," said Frank. "As you have overheard, we need a little more capital than what we actually have. I will remember your kind offer, and if we cannot figure it out as we hope I may speak to you on the subject later."

"I wish you would come right up to the house now and tell my Aunt Susie all about it," pressed Peter, urgently.

"I couldn't think of it," answered Frank. "No, you leave matters just as I suggest and we will see what may come of it."

"Say, Frank," whispered Pep, on fire with excitement, "you don't mean to think of encouraging this noodle; do you?"

"I want to get rid of him," answered Frank, and all hands were relieved to see the persistent Peter rise from his seat.

"Oh, say," he suddenly exclaimed—"I came for something, that's so. My aunt wants to see you, all three of you. Miss Porter gave her your names and addresses and she wouldn't rest until I had come down here. She wants you all to come to dinner to-morrow evening and she won't take no for an answer."

"Why, we may not be here then," said Frank.

"Oh, you must come," declared Peter, "now I have a chance to go in with you. I couldn't think of your not seeing her. Look here," and Peter winked and tried to look sly—"Aunt Susie is no tightwad. She is the most generous woman in the world. She's minded to give you fellows a fine meal and treat you like princes. She considers that you saved her life and she can't do too much for you. Say, on the quiet, I'll bet she makes you a present of fifty dollars apiece."

"What for?" demanded Frank.

"For getting to that burning boat and saving all hands, of course. Why, I wouldn't take the risk you did of being blown up for a thousand dollars."

"No, I don't think you would," announced Pep, bluntly.

"I'll tell you," went on their guest—"if you'll give me a tip on the side I'll work up Aunt Susie to a hundred dollars apiece. There, I know I can do it."

Frank bit his lip and tried to keep from losing his temper with this mean-spirited cad. Then he said with quiet dignity:

"I think you had better go, Mr. Carrington, and I shall expect you to tell your aunt that we were only too glad to do a trifling service for her. Please inform her, also, that I am quite certain we shall be too busy to accept her kind invitation for to-morrow evening; in fact, we may leave Seaside Park for our home at Fairlands early in the morning."

Dauntless Peter! you could not squelch that shallow nerve of his. In a trice he shouted out:

"Why! do you live at Fairlands?"

"Yes," nodded Frank, wondering what was coming next from this extraordinary youth.

"Then you know Greg Grayson?"

"Oh, yes," admitted Randy.

"I should think we did!" observed Pep, with a wry grimace.

"Why, then, we're regular friends," insisted Peter, acting as if he was about to embrace all hands. "He was my roommate at school. We were like twin brothers."

"Maybe that's the reason!" muttered Pep.

"His folks are big guns in Fairlands, just as we are here. Say, if you know Greg Grayson, that settles it. You just ask him if I ain't all right—up to snuff and all that—and if I wouldn't make a fine partner."

Frank managed to usher their persistent visitor from the room, all the way down the corridor the latter insisting that he was going to "put the proposition up to Aunt Susie" forthwith, and that they would hear from him on the morrow.

"Frank," exclaimed Pep, "it seems good to get rid of that fellow."

"A fine partner he'd make," observed Randy, with a snort.

"I am dreadfully sorry he overheard our plans," spoke Frank. "Of course it will soon be generally known if we decide to locate here; but this Peter may talk a lot of rubbish that might hurt us or start somebody else on our idea."

"And to think of his knowing Greg Grayson, and playing him off on us as a recommendation!" cried Pep.

"They make a good pair," added Randy. "Why, I'd give up the whole business before I would have either of them connected with our plans in any way."

"I wouldn't wonder if Mr. Jolly might happen along if we stay here a day or two longer," remarked Frank. "You know he was the first to suggest a look at Seaside Park with a view to business."

"That's so," said Randy. "Did you write to him, Frank?"

"Yes. You know when we closed up at Fairlands he said he would take a day or two visiting some relatives and looking over the movies business in the city."

"Ben Jolly told me he wasn't going to stay idle all summer. Nor let us do it, either," observed Pep. "He'll have something fresh to tell us when we see him."

"Well, when we left Fairlands I sent him a few lines telling him that we were going to look over the field here," said Frank. "That is why I think he may drop in on us."

"I wish he would," declared Randy. "Mr. Jolly knows so much about the business. What's the programme for to-morrow, Frank?"

"Why, I thought we would find out what it will cost us to move our traps here from Fairlands, the amount of the license fee for the show, the cost of a lot of electric wiring and current we will need if we locate at Seaside Park, how much it will cost us to live, and a lot of such details."

The boys had a wonderfully refreshing sleep in that high room pervaded with cool ocean breezes, and got up fully an hour later than they had planned. After Peter Carrington had left them the evening before they had strolled down the beach about nine o'clock to get an idea of the evening crowds. This filled them more than ever with ardor as to their prospective business undertaking.

"I say," Randy had observed, "don't you see, Frank, there aren't enough amusements to go around?"

"Yes," Frank had assented, "the crowds seem just in trim for some lively entertainment."

The chums dispatched a substantial breakfast at the restaurant. Then they started out on their second day's investigation of conditions and prospects at Seaside Park.

Frank made it a point to interview several owners of concessions along the beach. Those with whom he talked had attractions vastly inferior to the one the chums designed to operate, but the boys picked up many a suggestion and useful hint. It was shortly before noon when they sat down to rest under a tree in that part of the town given over to permanent residences and summer cottages. They began talking over the ever-present theme of their photo playhouse when there was an interruption.

Down the street there strolled leisurely a young man who made it a point to halt whenever he got in front of a house. There he would linger and begin a series of whistling exploits that made the air vibrate with the most ravishing melody.

"Say, just listen to that!" exclaimed Pep, in a pleased tone.

"It's one of those trick whistles," declared Randy.

"Then it's an extra fine one," said Pep.

"I think you are mistaken, boys," suggested Frank. "Those are real human notes—at least almost exact human imitations of bird tones."

"Well, then, the fellow must have a throat like a nightingale," asserted the enthusiastic Pep.

The active whistler deserved all the chums said about him. His repertoire seemed exhaustless. He confined himself to imitations of birds exclusively— and of only such birds as were native to the surrounding country.

He fairly filled the air with melody, and real birds in the trees and shrubbery about the handsome residences of the locality twittered, hopped about and responded in an echoing chorus to his expert call.

Little children came running out of yards to gaze in wonder and admiration at this unusual warbler. Even older folks watched and listened to him. The man turned a corner out of view of the motion picture chums, followed by quite a procession.

He had scarcely vanished before a high wagon such as is used to carry cooper's barrels turned slowly into the street. A slow old horse pulled it along. Its driver nimbly leaped from his seat. The moment he called out "Whoa!" to the horse and turned his face toward the chums, Pep Smith uttered a great shout.

"Why, fellows, see," he cried, in mingled glee and surprise—"it's Ben Jolly!"

CHAPTER V—THE BIRD HOUSE

Ben Jolly it was, more sprightly, more jolly-looking than ever, for he waved his hand with a genial smile to the children staring down the side street after the whistler. The other reached into the wagon. Instantly upon recognizing their old-time friend and helper the three chums started in his direction.

"Hi, there!" hailed Pep, while Randy waved his hand gaily and all hurried their gait.

"Well! well!" exclaimed Jolly, his face an expanding smile of welcome, extending both hands and greeting his friends in turn. "I expected to find you here and headed for here, but I did not expect to run across you so oddly."

"For mercy's sake, Mr. Jolly," burst forth Randy, staring in amazement at the wagon, "what in the world have you got there?"

"Why bird houses," replied Jolly.

"Bird houses?" repeated Pep, equally bewildered. "What are you doing with such a lot of bird houses?"

"Selling them, of course."

Frank himself was surprised and puzzled. The wagon contained half a dozen tiers of little box-like structures packed close. At one side was a heap of poles the size of display flag staffs. These poles were stout and heavy, painted white, and about twelve feet in length. The houses were about two feet high and as wide. They were painted white, like the poles, and were exact models of a broad, low colonial house, even to the veranda. The roof was painted red, there was an imitation chimney and a double open doorway in front trimmed with green. All around this miniature house were little apertures representing windows.

A neater, more inviting little bird house for a garden could not well be imagined. As Jolly took a sample from the wagon the little children flocked about him on tiptoe of curiosity. There were admiring "Oh's!" and "Ah's!" "Ain't they cute!" "What cunning little houses!" and "Oh, mister! are they for sale?" "What do they cost?"

"If you will excuse me while I make a demonstration," observed Jolly, "I'll explain what it's all about."

"What a rare fellow he is!" remarked Randy to his companions, as they stepped aside.

"The same busy, happy, good-natured friend of everybody," returned Frank, with genuine feeling.

If there was a being in the world the motion picture chums had reason to feel kindly toward it was this same Ben Jolly. A free wanderer, taking things easy, tramping flower-fringed country roads, making his way, willing to meet any task that came along, Ben Jolly had dropped into their life at the critical moment when they were discussing the prospects of their first motion picture show at Fairlands.

Ben had been a Jack-of-all-trades and knew a little something about pretty nearly everything. Particularly he knew a good deal about the movies. He gave the boys advice and suggestions that enabled them to buy their first outfit at a bargain and the day the show opened appeared with an old piano which he had induced a rich relative to buy. From that time on Ben Jolly furnished the music for the Wonderland photo playhouse and, as told in our first volume, was the means of unearthing a plot against the father of Frank Durham, whereby he had been swindled out of a small estate.

Jolly took a sample bird house under each arm and entered the first yard he came to, the interested children keeping him close company. He came out of the first house with only one bird house, he came out of the second with none. Along the block he visited on both sides of the street Jolly disposed of just eleven of the attractive little miniature domiciles, distributed poles later to each purchaser and rejoined the boys.

"Now, then," he said, briskly, placing a little roll of banknotes in a well-filled wallet, "how are you and what are the prospects?"

"Excellent," declared Randy. "See here, though, Mr. Jolly, will you kindly explain this new business of yours?"

"Simply a side line," replied Jolly, in a gay, offhand manner.

"But where did you ever pick up that rig and that lot of odd truck?" challenged Pep.

"I picked up better than that," retorted Jolly, cheerily. "I ran across the finest advance agent in the business—and here he comes. You knew him once, but under his stage name of Hal Pope. He's Mr. Hal Vincent now."

At that moment the whistler came into view, having circled the block. As he approached, Frank's face expressed pleased surprise.

"Why," exclaimed Pep, "it's our friend the ventriloquist."

"So it is," echoed Randy.

"Glad to meet you again," said Hal Vincent, and there was an all-around handshaking. "You're all looking fine and I hear you're prosperous."

"Not so much so that we could afford to hire you for our programme at Fairlands, as we would like to do, Mr. Vincent," replied Frank, with a smile.

Pep began to grin as he looked at Vincent, and the memory of their first meeting was reviewed. Then he chuckled and finally he broke out into a ringing guffaw.

"Thinking of my first and only appearance at that auction where you bought your movies outfit?" inquired Vincent, with a smile.

"Will we ever forget it?" cried Randy. "I tell you, Mr. Vincent, if you hadn't made the auctioneer believe that two innocent bystanders were bidding against each other with your ventriloquism, and gained time until Frank arrived, we would never have gotten into the motion picture business."

"It worked finely; didn't it?" answered Vincent.

"I ran across Hal at Tresco, about thirty miles from here," narrated Ben Jolly. "He was counting the ties in the direction of New York, having left the dummies he uses in his stunts on the stage for meals and lodging."

"Yes, I was about all that was left of the Consolidated Popular Amusement Corporation," put in Vincent. "I was glad to meet an old friend like Ben. He told me there was the shadow of a chance that you might start in at Seaside Park and wanted me to come along with him. Then we ran across the outfit here," and the speaker nodded toward the wagon and its contents.

"That was my brilliant idea," added Jolly. "I call it a rare stroke of luck, the way we ran across the outfit."

"How?" projected Pep, vastly curious.

"Well, a carpenter in a little town we came through had got crippled. The doctor told him he wouldn't get around without crutches for six months. He was a lively, industrious old fellow and couldn't bear to be idle. Had a lot of waste lumber and worked it up into dog houses. There weren't many dogs in the town, so his sale was limited. Then the bird house idea came along. The carpenter got the local paper to print a lot about the birds, the merry birds, that sing about our door——"

"That—sing—about—our—door!" echoed a slow, deep bass, apparently away up in a high tree near by, and the boys knew that their gifted ventriloquist friend was exercising his talents.

"The carpenter," proceeded Jolly, "hired a lot of boys to go forth on his mission of kindness to our feathery songsters. The campaign went ahead until nearly everybody wanting a bird house got one. Our friend found himself with some two hundred of the little structures left on his hands. He had overstocked the market, with a big surplus left on his hands. When we came along it was a sign in front of his place that attracted our attention. It read: 'These fine bird houses and a capable horse, wagon, and harness for sale for a mere song.'

"Anything odd always catches me, so I interviewed the old man. It seemed that he had received word only that day that a relative in another part of the country had left him a farm. He wanted to realize quick and he offered me the bird house outfit and the rig all for fifty dollars. I had only thirty-eight dollars, and he took that and gave me his new address. The arrangement was that if I was lucky in getting rid of the bird houses I was to send him the balance. If I didn't he was willing to charge it up to profit and loss. He'll get that balance," announced Jolly, with a satisfied smile.

"It looks so, judging from your sales of the last half-hour," remarked Frank.

"What do you get for the little houses, Mr. Jolly?" inquired Randy.

"A dollar apiece. I don't sell them, though—not a bit of it," exclaimed Ben Jolly, modestly. "It's Hal. You ought to hear his whole repertoire—orioles, thrushes, mourning doves, nightingales, mocking birds. He infuses the neighborhood with the melody and I slide in with the practical goods. And that rig—remember the noise wagon at Fairlands, Pep Smith?"

"Do I?" cried Pep, in a gloating way—"I should say I did!"

The "noise wagon" had been introduced in connection with the photo playhouse at Fairlands and had become a novel institution with the inhabitants. A wagon enclosed with canvas, bearing announcements of existing and coming film features, was provided with a big bass drum, bells, huge board clappers and some horns—all operated by pedals under the driver's feet.

"You see this new rig of mine would work in on the same basis here," proceeded Jolly. "If not, I can get more for the outfit than I paid for it, anyway. Now then, Durham, where can we find you this evening?"

"Why not sooner?" suggested the impetuous Pep. "We've a great lot to tell you, Mr. Jolly."

"And I'm anxious to hear it all," declared Jolly, "but we've got our stock to get rid of. Nothing like keeping at it when you've made a good beginning; and this town starts out promising-like."

Frank now decided that he would remain over at Seaside Park for another day at least. The appearance of Ben Jolly somehow infused all hands with renewed vim and cheerfulness. The chums were glad also to meet Hal Vincent. He had done them a big favor in the past and they realized that he could be of considerable advantage to them in the future in case they located at Seaside Park.

Vincent had the reputation of being an accomplished all-around entertainer. He was an expert ventriloquist and parlor magician, liked the boys and had told Frank on the occasion of their first meeting that he would be glad to go on their programme at any time for a very moderate compensation.

Ben Jolly burst in upon his young friends with his usual bustle and buoyancy about six o'clock that evening. He merrily chinked a pocket full of silver and was all ready for what might next come along, and eager to tackle it.

"Left Hal finishing one of the few full meals he has had since his show broke up," reported Jolly. "Got rid of the last one of the bird houses—and, see here, Frank," and the volatile speaker exhibited a comfortable-looking roll of bank notes. "That was a fine speculation, the way it turned out, and leaves me quite in funds. Now then, what's the programme?"

Frank became serious at once and all the others as well. He told his loyal friend all about their plans and hopes. Jolly shook his head soberly when Frank produced some figures showing that the amount necessary to operate a new photo playhouse was beyond their ready means.

"I've got nearly one hundred dollars you are welcome to," reported Jolly promptly, "but that's about my limit. You see, when I got the money to buy that piano and the 'noise wagon' I practically sold my prospects for a last mess of pottage. I'm willing to pitch in and live 'most any way to give the new show a start, but when it comes to raising the extra five hundred dollars needed, I'm afraid I can't help you much."

Randy looked glum at this, and Pep was almost crying. Ben Jolly sat chewing a toothpick vigorously, his thinking cap on.

"Perhaps we had better give up the idea of coming to Seaside Park until we are a little stronger in a money way——" Frank had begun, when there was an interruption.

"Someone to see Mr. Frank Durham," announced a bellboy, appearing in the open doorway.

Frank arose from his chair promptly and went out into the corridor.

"In the ladies' parlor, sir," added the bellboy, and Frank went down the stairs, wondering who this unexpected visitor could be.

CHAPTER VI—A FRIEND IN NEED

Frank Durham entered the ladies' parlor of the hotel to see a stout, dressy woman arise, joined by a girlish companion. He recognized both at once. They were the persons he had taken aboard the launch from the burning motor boat the afternoon before.

"This is Mr. Durham," spoke Miss Porter, and she smiled in a friendly way at our hero, while her companion extended her bejeweled hand with a decided show of welcome.

"I was so overcome by that explosion," said Mrs. Carrington, "that I just got a glimpse of you. Then that ridiculous fainting away! I have thanked Miss Porter a dozen times for having had the foresight to obtain your name and that of your brave young comrades. Now then, Mr. Durham, if you please, sit down and give an account of yourself."

"In what way, madam?" asked Frank, with an embarrassed smile, and flushing at the compliment conveyed.

"Why have you not accepted our invitation to come up to the house, as I requested?" demanded Mrs. Carrington, pretending to be very severe.

"I certainly appreciated your kindness in thinking of me," replied Frank; "but I have been very much occupied with business and did not know yesterday how long I would remain at Seaside Park. Then, too, some friends arrived this afternoon."

"I am used to being obeyed, young man," Mrs. Carrington, with a playful frown. "I have no doubt, though, that I sent a blundering messenger. Oh, that Peter of mine! I never know how to place him. He came back perfectly wild over going into the motion picture business with you. He has been tormenting me all day long about it. I have told him decidedly that I should not encourage him in any way.

"To tell you the truth, Mr. Durham, Peter is a sad failure at anything that requires application and work. I would not do you the injustice of having you hampered by a person who has no business training and does not know the value of money. The fact is, Peter has been a great cross to me of late, and I am now in correspondence with a military school, with the idea of getting him where a year's discipline may do him some good."

Frank had not for a moment seriously entertained the thought of taking Peter Carrington into partnership. He felt immensely relieved, however, to find that his visitor did not press that phase of the subject.

"I have come, first and foremost," went on the fussy but good-natured lady, "to thank you for what you did for us. When I think of how near we were to drowning or burning up it makes me shudder! My friends, who happened to see your picture in this morning's paper——"

"My picture?" exclaimed Frank, in bewilderment. "What picture, Mrs. Carrington?"

"Why," cried Mrs. Carrington, "he actually is so modest he hasn't realized what a hero he has been! I refer to the splendid account of your bravery in the Brenton Daily News."

Brenton was the nearest city, about twenty miles from Seaside Park. Frank began to get a faint glimmering of the situation now. The reporter who had snap-shotted him with his camera from the pier must have sent his story to the paper Mrs. Carrington mentioned.

"I think I have the clipping about the rescue," observed Miss Porter, groping in her hand bag while her merry eyes twinkled as she observed the increasing embarrassment of Frank. "Yes, here it is."

Frank only glanced at the clipping that was held forward for his inspection. He could not help but notice the glowing head line; "A Signal Act of Bravery," and observe that a very fair picture of himself in the launch was shown.

"You can have it, Mr. Durham," continued his mischievous tormentor with a smile. "Your friends are named also in the paper and they may not dislike honest praise, as you seem to do."

"Now then," broke in Mrs. Carrington, in her self-assertive way, "let me say what I specially came down here to say. Oh, I was telling about my friends. They have fairly overwhelmed me with congratulations over my fortunate escape."

"Yes, and some of them who saw the newspaper account said—what was it, Mrs. Carrington? You must tell Mr. Durham," declared the younger woman.

"About the handsome picture and what a sensible, thoughtful young man our rescuer must be?"

"Oh, Mrs. Carrington," pleaded Frank. "I beg of you!—it is I who am being overwhelmed now. You will make me so vain I will really begin to think I did something of consequence. Why, there isn't a young fellow anywhere who wouldn't hasten to help ladies in distress."

"Don't belittle what you did," said Mrs. Carrington, and her face and tone grew very serious. "You did so much of consequence, Mr. Durham, and you did it so manfully and nobly that I would not think of affronting you with any offer of a reward. I fancy I read you deeper than you think as to that feature. I will say this, however, and I came here especially to say it, that I am your true friend and I am anxious to help you and your young companions in a practical, useful way."

"You are very, very kind to say what you do," said Frank earnestly.

"Let me be really kind," suggested Mrs. Carrington, "and I shall be satisfied. My nephew has told me enough about your business plans to convince me that you are at a critical point in your career, where a little capital may be everything to you. I am a wealthy woman, Mr. Durham. I do not wish to offer you a gift. Simply as a business woman who has confidence in you, let me know about your affairs and help you in a business way."

Frank's head drooped. The boy who never flinched from pain or fear was so deeply moved by the friendly interest of this kind-hearted woman, that he could not keep back a long-drawn sigh of appreciation and gratitude.

"You make me think of my own kind mother," said Frank quite brokenly. "It is worth living to find such friends."

"You dear boy!" cried Mrs. Carrington, placing a hand on Frank's arm, "I can imagine what a lovely mother you must have and for her sake you must let me help you along in your business enterprise. Come, Mr. Durham, explain your needs to me and let me co-operate with you."

The invitation was irresistible. Long since Frank had calculated all the risks and chances of success in his new enterprise and had decided that it could scarcely fail.

"Mrs. Carrington," he said in a straightforward way, "I would not allow any person to invest money in a business where there was the remotest risk of loss. We lack a few hundred dollars to start a photo playhouse at Seaside Park in the right way. If you feel in a position to advance it or become responsible for what we need, I wish to secure you so that in case the venture goes wrong we will be the only losers."

"I not only feel willing to assist you," said Mrs. Carrington, "but I insist upon it. It is very simple—how much capital do you require? Have you my check book in your hand bag, Miss Porter?"

"No! no! no!" interrupted Frank urgently, "you must not think of doing such a thing as that, Mrs. Carrington. It isn't business, you see. If you have some agent or lawyer who will act for you, that will be the best way."

The kind lady looked disappointed at the suggestion. In her free-hearted way she wished to trust Frank without restriction. He saw that her feelings were hurt and he hastened to say:

"My partners will feel ever so much better to have everything arranged in a regular way and set down in black and white."

"Very well, have your own way, Mr. Durham," said the lady, "only promise to come to me if you have any troubles or further lack of funds."

"Oh, we shall not," declared Frank, brightening with courage and confidence as he saw all obstructions to the success of the new show removed; and before he realized it, in his quick, vivid way he was reciting his plans and prospects in detail. Frank told more than he had started out to do, for the reason that every time he paused his auditors plied him with new questions and urged him on with his story.

"How very, very interesting," commented Mrs. Carrington.

"It is simply delightful!" declared Miss Porter, with sparkling eyes. "Oh, dear! it must be such a splendid thing to be a boy!"

"I must see your young friends," insisted Mrs. Carrington. "I owe them sincere thanks for their part in the rescue, and wish to tell them so."

There was nothing for it but that Frank should go for his chums. Randy was naturally bashful in the presence of strange ladies, but Pep was "all there." Both Mrs. Carrington and Miss Porter were interested in the lively lad whom they attracted from the start and made Pep feel completely at home with his impetuous, original ways and remarks.

The boys promised to call upon Mrs. Carrington as soon as they got settled at Seaside Park. Then all three escorted the visitors to an automobile waiting at the curb. Beside the chauffeur they found Peter Carrington seated. He nodded familiarly to the chums. Then he caught Pep's eye.

With an air of great importance and a quick glance at his aunt and her companion, as if making sure that they were not observing him, he placed a finger to his lips.

"S-st!" he uttered, and winked in an altogether mysterious manner at Pep Smith.

"'S-st!'" repeated Pep, as the machine started on its way—"now what in the world does Peter Carrington mean by 'S-st?'"

CHAPTER VII—BUSINESS BOYS

"I hope I did right, fellows," said Frank.

"You never do any other way," declared Randy Powell loyally.

"Exactly my sentiments," echoed the impetuous Pep Smith. "You'll say so, too; won't you, Mr. Jolly?"

"I don't have to say it," retorted Ben Jolly quickly, "you all know I think it. You're a man of business, Frank Durham, and a Philadelphia lawyer couldn't have conducted this deal in a neater, squarer way."

"Thank you," acknowledged Frank, slightly flustered at the compliments of the coterie of friends about him.

The new photo playhouse at Seaside Park was a certainty. When the boys came down from their rooms at the hotel the morning after the visit from Mrs. Carrington and her companion, the clerk called to Frank as he was leaving the place.

"Telephone message for you last night, Mr. Durham," he said. "It came about ten o'clock and as it was not urgent and I did not wish to disturb you, I thought I would keep it until this morning."

The speaker handed a memorandum slip to Frank. It read: "Attorney William Slade, on request of Mrs. Carrington, would like to see you in the morning."

Frank showed the memorandum to Randy and Pep. The chums at once realized what it meant. It evinced the determination of the strong-willed Mrs. Carrington to have her own way. In fact the boys had come to the conclusion that she should do so. With Ben Jolly, up in their room after their visitors had departed, they had gone over the entire proposition in detail.

"You would be foolish to allow this chance to get the capital you need in this business go by," advised Jolly. "Putting aside the fact that this lady feels indebted to you, her offer is fair, square and business-like."

Frank thought over the affair in its every phase long after Randy and Pep had gone to sleep. Jolly and Vincent had gotten a free shelter for their rig and left the hotel to sleep in the wagon.

"Used to that, you know—the only way in the world to live," asserted Jolly, and then they made an arrangement to meet in the morning. The 'phone message at once set things in motion. The chums had breakfast, Frank learned the address of Mr. Slade, and about nine o'clock started for his office, which was located over the bank of the town.

"You had better meet Mr. Jolly, as we agreed," directed Frank to his companions.

"Where will you pick us up again?" questioned Randy.

"Why, I think I shall not be with this Mr. Slade more than an hour," explained Frank.

"Say, then," suggested Pep, "suppose we go over to the empty store you're thinking of turning into a motion picture show and hang around there?"

"That empty store has a remarkable fascination for you, Pep," smiled Frank.

"You bet it has," confessed Pep. "Mr. Jolly is just as wild over it. I shouldn't wonder if he was looking it over carefully the first thing this morning."

"Very well," said Frank, "we will all meet there say at eleven o'clock."

Then Frank had gone on his way to report at the empty store half an hour earlier than he expected. He found his chums and Ben Jolly anxiously awaiting him. Vincent had remained with the horse and wagon at the barn.

There were some old chairs at the rear of the vacant building, and Mr. Morton invited them to make free use of them. It was quite a business conclave that grouped together while Frank told his story. It was clear and simple. Mrs. Carrington had instructed her attorney to advance up to one thousand dollars to Frank and his friends as needed.

"I insisted that we give the lady a bill of sale of all our belongings as security," explained Frank. "The lawyer laughed at me. 'You don't know a good thing when you see it,' he said. 'Perhaps not,' I told him; 'but I know an honorable way to protect those who have confidence in me, as far as I can.' Well, anyhow, I made him write out a memorandum of the whole transaction and signed a bill of sale. Was I going too fast in setting myself up as the one man of this very enterprising firm? I hope I did exactly right."

And then followed the hearty sanction of Jolly and the boys to all Frank had done.

"I'm only a sort of drifter-in," observed Jolly, "so what I say is only out of friendly interest. I would advise that just one of the firm take the responsibility, if he's willing, on the lease and in all business dealings. It simplifies things, you see."

"It's got to be Frank, then," spoke Randy.

"It will always be Frank," echoed Pep. "He's the brains of the business; isn't he?"

"I don't like the way you put it as to your being a drifter-in, as you call it, Mr. Jolly," said Frank. "If it wasn't for you I am afraid the Fairlands venture wouldn't have amounted to much."

"Sho!" derided Jolly modestly.

"It's true. You had your way about that and drew just as little money as you could. Of course that was an experiment, and I let you have your own way. Now we are on a broader basis and I'm going to have mine."

"Are you?" challenged Jolly, with twinkling eyes.

"Yes, sir, I am. I shall make a definite new deal all around."

"Will you?" said Jolly.

"Don't you doubt it. You've been a staunch, helpful friend and it's equal partners, if we come to Seaside Park."

"That is, you think you are going to make a business man of me?"

"You've been one all along," vociferated Pep. "Why, that noise wagon idea alone——"

"A freak," interrupted Jolly, but Frank was resolute and it was settled that their interesting friend should have a quarter interest in the profits of the new venture.

Frank called Mr. Morton into their confab. He explained to him precisely their plans and the extent of their capital.

"Mrs. Carrington backing you; eh?" he observed. "That makes you pretty solid, if you only knew it, young man, although I had about made up my mind to accept you as a tenant without any guarantee. Shall we call it settled—you lease the premises until October first, pay me the first month's rent before you come in and give me your word that you won't break the lease?"

"I wouldn't take the place on any other arrangement," said Frank.

"It's settled, then," said their landlord, and Pep followed him as he went to the window where the "To Rent" sign was placed, removed it and began to tear it up. Pep was pretty near dancing. If they had been given a palace he could not have been more pleased.

"S-st!" sounded a sudden hail and the ubiquitous and mysterious Peter Carrington came into evidence just outside the open doorway.

"Hello!" challenged Pep, who could not repress his dislike for a fellow who had played the eavesdropper and left a relative to the risk of drowning. "What you snooping around for?"

"Wanted to see you."

"All right," nodded Pep carelessly. "You don't have to 'S-st' at me regularly to get my attention, though. What's on your mind?"

"I see the rent sign is down."

"Yes," proclaimed Pep grandly, "we have leased the premises."

"Well, I'm dead gone on being a partner. Aunt Susie discourages me, but I don't care for that. There's an uncle of mine over in Brenton who says he will back me if the thing shows up good, and I want to have a talk with you fellows——"

"Say, we have all the capital we need," announced Pep.

"Oh, you have?"

"A new partner just came in."

"Huh!" snorted Peter. "Say, you don't mean my aunt?"

"She is not a partner, no."

Peter looked abashed, then disappointed, then angry.

"'Tain't fair!" he declared.

"What isn't fair?"

"I spoke first and I deserve to have a show."

"No one asked you to speak first; did he?" propounded Pep bluntly.

This staggered Peter. He stood thinking deeply. Then he looked Pep over and seemed to be studying something.

"See here," he said with a half-cunning expression in his face, "I suppose you know a heap about the movies?"

"Oh, tolerable, tolerable," responded Pep, who did indeed think so.

"And you remember Greg Grayson, of Fairlands?"

"I have a perfectly clear memory of Mr. Gregory Grayson," answered Pep, his nostrils dilating, but Peter was too obtuse to read between the lines.

"Well, I've got an idea," chuckled Peter. "Anybody has a right to start a movies show; haven't they?"

"If they want to, I suppose."

"Well, since I can't make a deal with that Durham, I'm going it on my own hook. I can raise the money; Greg's father is rich and he can help. All we need is someone who knows the practical end of the business. Say, you come in with us and I'll give you double what you expect to make with those fellows there."

Pep doubled up a fist. He was angry clear through. At a mere hint of disloyalty to his famous friends he took fire. He gave Peter a push.

"You get out!" he ordered staunchly.

"Hey?" goggled Peter.

"And stay out!"

"Humph!"

Peter got to a safe distance. Then he shook his fist at Pep.

"Say," he snarled, "you've waked up the wrong customer. I've given you the chance of your life and you've turned me down and insulted me. I'll show you something. Greg Grayson and I will put a spoke in the wheel of that Frank Durham and your whole precious crowd; see of we don't!"

CHAPTER VIII—KIDNAPPED

"If I had our old piano here," said Ben Jolly, "there's one tune I'd play for all it's worth."

"What is that, Mr. Jolly?" inquired Frank Durham.

"'Home, Sweet Home.'"

The staunch friend of the motion picture chums waved his hand like a showman proudly exhibiting wares. He had a smiling and enthusiastic audience. Everybody was smiling, even Hal Vincent, who had no particular interest in the new photo playhouse. Frank's face was beaming, Randy looked his delight and Pep uttered the words, with unction:

"It's simply great!"

Two days had made considerable difference in the situation at Seaside Park. All hands had entered with enthusiasm into the proposition of starting in on the new deal, with the certainty in view of sufficient capital to finance them for at least two months ahead. The chums spent so many delightful hours figuring, planning, and mapping out details that Randy got to talking in his sleep, and Pep aroused all hands by screaming out in the midst of a nightmare in which he had started a photo playhouse in China, and the natives had mobbed him when a film showed one of their favorite mandarins being carried away in an airship.

It was Jolly, however—bustling, practical Ben Jolly—who had won the laurels on the present occasion. When the vacant store had been used, at the rear was a temporary kitchen. This was a frail structure set on stilts, but roomy and just the thing for summer occupancy. Jolly was a natural born trader. It seemed that he found some difficulty in disposing of the old horse and wagon for cash. Finally, however, he came across a dealer in second hand furniture. Jolly had got the idea in his head of cutting down living expenses and utilizing the old kitchen tacked on to the store building.

The chums were down at the hotel that afternoon and Jolly planned a grand surprise for them. It was now, upon their arrival at the playhouse building, that the pleasure and praise of the motion picture chums hailed him.

No one could have failed to approve of the wonderful transformation Jolly had made in a bare, cheerless lumber room. He had traded to good advantage. There was a substantial table, a half dozen chairs, a cupboard, a gas stove, a complete outfit of culinary utensils, dishes and table cutlery, neat curtains for the windows and drapery dividing the room in two parts, and one side section again into two compartments.

In each of these were three cots, a table and a bureau. The cots had double equipment of sheets and blankets, worn but attractive rugs covered the floor, and there were several pictures on the walls. It was no wonder that Pep Smith burst forth in his usual responsive way with the declaration:

"It's simply great!"

"When you come to think that I got all those traps and forty dollars in cash to boot for that impossible old rig of ours," observed Jolly, "you will see that I made a very interesting dicker. What do you say, Durham; we can make a neat cut in expenses, eh?"

"Why, it makes easy the hardest part of our whole proposition," declared Frank.

"Yes, and here we can always be right on the spot," spoke Randy.

"I'm something of a cook," boasted Jolly. "I don't say I could make bread or pie, but as to common, everyday food, an occasional strawberry shortcake, or even doughnuts—well, you stock up with the supplies and I'll promise to do my best."

"It's just fine," voted Pep. "The sleeping rooms look right across to the ocean and there's a splendid sweep of air with all these openings. It will be cool and comfortable on the very hottest nights. I'll wash all the dishes, Mr. Jolly, and set the table, and all that."

"Oh, we shall get on famously, I am sure of that," observed Frank with keen satisfaction.

The boys decided that they would at once move their traps from the hotel and make permanent headquarters at their home base. They had their first meal in their new quarters that evening.

"You have certainly given us a royal meal, Mr. Jolly," declared Frank, as beefsteak, fried potatoes, bakery biscuit, and coffee and a really creditable corn starch pudding went the rounds.

"Sorry I've got to leave you," remarked Vincent. "I'd ask nothing better than to camp right here for the rest of the season."

"Then why not do it?" inquired the ready Pep.

"Yes, if you care to take pot luck with us till we get fairly on our feet, you can certainly help us along with all your varied accomplishments, Mr. Vincent," declared Frank.

"I've got that in mind," explained Vincent, "but I must get to New York first. You see, the show I was with that broke up owes me money. I want to see if I can't get something out of the wreck and I want to call on the backers of the proposition. I'd better get to the city while I have the partnership profits Jolly has been good enough to say I have earned on that bird house speculation. If I don't it will melt away."

"I say," here put in Jolly, "why don't you and Durham go together? As it's arranged, Durham, you have got to put in a day or two arranging for what new equipment we need and the film service."

"That is true," replied Frank, "and Mr. Vincent knows so much about the motion picture business his advice and help would be of great benefit to me."

"I do know the ropes among the movies pretty well," said Vincent. "I will be more than glad to take you the rounds and see that you get the very best service and figures, Mr. Durham."

"And I am to go back to Fairlands and arrange about moving what we want of the old outfit?" inquired Jolly.

"I think that is the best arrangement, yes," assented Frank. "Randy and Pep must stay here to look after the place and receive what I may ship and what you send on. Then, before we start, the three of us must run down to Fairlands to see the folks."

Everything was settled on that basis. It would take about ten days to get the place fitted up as the boys wanted it, Mr. Morton told them. In the meantime there were many little things that needed to be done in which two handy lads like Randy and Pep might help. They and Jolly went to the train to see Frank and Vincent off the next morning. Two hours later Ben Jolly took a train in another direction, bound for Fairlands and carrying messages from the boys to their home folks and friends.

Part of the fixing up of the store room Mr. Morton had agreed to do at his own expense. There were, however, innumerable details that fell to the lot of the boys themselves. There were rolls of matting to buy for the center aisle, and the stage was to be built under Randy's supervision. They had decided to use the old name, "Wonderland," so as to utilize the ornate electric sign they had at Fairlands, and Pep was given charge of having this same name placed in a decorative way on the two front windows.

Nobody could work with Randy and Pep without coming under the influence of their sunshiny natures. Randy was willing, accommodating and tireless when he liked a job. Pep was no laggard, either, and in addition he kept up such a lively chatter and made so many funny remarks that he had Mr. Morton grinning half the time.

The result was that not only did the owner of the place do all that he had agreed to do, but did it just as the boys wanted. Then again when it came to things not in his contract, he supplied the material voluntarily and ended up by helping the boys at their tasks.

At the end of three days Randy and Pep prided themselves on having accomplished wonders. They had added several genuine comforts to their living quarters at the rear and had pretty well spread the news over Seaside Park that a first-class photo playhouse was soon to be opened.

A letter came from Frank Saturday morning. It told of his busy hours in the city and referred to Vincent as a splendid help in introducing him among the motion picture supply men. He sent on a bundle of film and song posters from which Pep could scarcely keep his hands. Frank mentioned some of the movies accessories he had purchased and told of some novel features in the way of films for which he had contracted.

"I tell you, Pep, we're in for the best or nothing this time; eh?" questioned Randy, almost as much excited as his chums over the prospects of the new Wonderland.

"Oh, I'm 'way up in the clouds all of the time," piped Pep. "Why, I'll feel like a girl just going into society. I'm going to call it a short day and quit. There are some groceries to order, so I'll attend to that and we'll take in the beach this evening."

"Yes, we've earned a little recreation, I think," agreed Randy.

Pep started off, whistling like some happy lark. It was then five o'clock in the afternoon and he was due to return in half an hour. Double that time passed on, however, yet he did not appear.

"Wonder why Pep doesn't show up?" ruminated Randy. "It's time he did, as we wanted to get an early start."

At half past six Randy was nervous and a little put out. At seven o'clock he put on his cap and started to lock up to go in quest of his missing comrade.

Just as he came out on the broad planking leading from the boardwalk to the entrance to the store, a man hailed him. He was a stout, lumbering old fellow whom Randy had seen before.

"Hi!" he hailed, "you remember me; don't you?"

"Why yes," nodded Randy. "You are the man Mr. Jolly traded his rig with for our furniture."

"That's it," nodded the man. "I say, I thought I'd come and tell you. It was near my place that the accident happened."

"What accident?" challenged Randy sharply.

"Automobile—that young fellow that's joshing and jollying all the time——"

"You mean Pep—Pepperill Smith?" asked Randy.

"That's him, I remember hearing Jolly call him by that name. Well, it was him that got hurt and——"

"Hurt!" cried Randy, alarmed at the word—"When? How? Where?"

"About an hour ago, by an automobile in front of my place," was the reply.

"Was he—was Pep seriously hurt?" faltered Randy.

"Not but what he could walk and sass the chauffeur, and all that; but I reckon one hand was pretty badly crushed. The reason I came to tell you was, that isn't all of it. From what I hear he is kidnapped."

CHAPTER IX—PEP IN CLOVER

"Kidnapped!" repeated Randy, in a hollow tone.

The furniture man nodded his head assentingly. He was big and fat and had evidently come in a hurry. He had been blunt, but confused in telling his story. Now he took a long breath to begin again.

Randy felt his heart sink. Everything had been going so well that the sudden news of an interruption to their buoyant progress chilled him through sheer contrast. He fancied all kinds of mishaps, and, seizing his visitor by the sleeve, pulled it in a worried way.

"Tell me all about it—quick," he demanded.

"Thought I had, but I guess you didn't get it straight. This Pep of yours was passing my place when I heard a woman shriek a bit ahead. She had left her child in a baby carriage while she went into a dry goods store. There came a whiff of wind down the street just as she came out. I don't wonder she hollered out, for that baby carriage was shooting across the street like a feather in a tornado."

"But—Pep?" urged Randy, breathlessly. "What of him?"

"He saw it in a flash. The woman stood motionless and screaming. This Pep made a sprint. I never saw anything done so splendidly. In a flash he slid over the pavement—just seemed to fly over the street, making for that baby carriage. No wonder he hurried and no wonder the woman screamed, for exactly at that instant a great red touring car came tearing around the corner. It held the chauffeur and a fine looking old gentleman, who just rose up in his seat with a yell as he saw that baby carriage directly in the path of the machine.

"There wasn't even time for the chauffeur to move the wheel. I actually shut my eyes, thinking the smash was bound to come. I don't know how the lad did it, but when I opened them, just cold with horror, there he was lying on the ground and the baby carriage spinning safe and sound across the street."

"How badly was Pep hurt?" inquired Randy, his face pale with suspense.

"I heard someone in the crowd say his wrist was broken. It seems, at the risk of his own life, he had made that dash for the baby carriage and given it a push out of the way of the auto just as it was pouncing down upon it."

"Where is Pep now?" asked Randy.

"Why, that is the queer part of it. The passenger in the machine jumped out and picked him up. He lifted him into the auto. He didn't seem to want to go with the man, but they speeded up and I supposed they were going to bring him here, or to the nearest doctor, or the hospital. A police officer came up right after the accident on a motorcycle. He made some inquiries, took some notes and went away again. Just now he came back and said that he could find no trace of machine or boy, and that he had learned that the auto had been driven out of town on the west road as fast as it could go. Don't you see—kidnapped!"

"I don't!" cried Randy almost frantically, "Wasn't it enough that they ran him down, without carrying him away nobody knows where? Oh, I must get straight on his track—I must find Pep!"

"The police didn't," suggested the furniture man.

"I don't care for that—I will!"

"Mebbe I'd better give you my address," said his visitor. "There's been several accidents here lately. It's mostly tourists passing through the town who are reckless about how they drive—rich old fellows who don't value life or limb, and get out of the way fast as they can when they've done any damage. I suppose the man who owns the machine that hurt your friend had heard of how one or two before him had been arrested and fined and forced to pay heavy damages, and just thought he'd grab up the lad and get him and himself out of the way before any investigation was made."

"It's shameful!" exclaimed Randy, wrought up now to the highest pitch of excitement and indignation. "Poor Pep! He may be suffering tortures and all those inhuman wretches think about is getting clear of being found out. I'll find him—I'll run down his kidnappers and bring them to account, even if the police can't."

The excited Randy did not even wait for the furniture man, but ran down the boardwalk and then in the direction of the man's store fast as he could. There was not much to learn there outside of what he already knew. His next call was at the police station. He was incensed at the indifference of the officers. They had investigated the accident as far as required, they claimed. The injured boy had been taken out of their jurisdiction and that seemed to lead them to believe that it ended their responsibility.

Randy knew the direction the red automobile had taken. He proceeded to a livery garage where motorcycles were on rent, and made himself known. He was well up in running the machine and was soon speeding on the trail of his missing chum, as he supposed and hoped. The west road out of Seaside

Park was the best in the section. It ran to Brenton and beyond that to the large cities. There was every reason to believe that the kidnappers, if such they were, would favor a smooth, easily traversed highway over inferior dirt and stone roads that ran parallel.

Randy stopped at the first little town he came to and made some inquiries, but they availed him nothing. Five miles further on, however, he got a clue. Here were crossroads and a "Roadside Rest," a general halting place for road-men. Several autos were in view, their occupants taking lunch in a pavilion near the hotel or walking about stretching their limbs.

A man who wore a banded cap and a close fitting coat flitted around here and there in an important way, and Randy decided he must be a sort of major domo about the place.

"I would like to inquire about an automobile that passed or stopped here within the past hour," spoke Randy, approaching this man.

"Where from? What number?" inquired the latter.

"I don't know," explained Randy, "but I will give you the best description I can from heresay. It was a big red car, and besides the chauffeur and passenger there was a boy about my age who had got his arm hurt——"

"Oh, I know now," interrupted the man—"you mean Colonel Tyson's car. They stopped to get a wet towel soaked in ice water to wrap around the boy's wrist, I fancy, for he was holding one arm and seemed in pain."

"Yes, yes—that is my friend," declared Randy hastily. "Which way did the machine go?"

"To Brenton, of course, where it belongs."

"Then you know its owner?"

"Everybody knows him—Tyson, the millionaire. Used to be a big bond man in New York City."

"Thank you," said Randy and was off on his travels again. "I hope Pep isn't hurt badly," he mused. "He doesn't seem to be from what I hear; but why is this rich old fellow running away with him?"

It was quite late in the evening when Randy reached Brenton. He felt easier, now that he seemed sure of locating his chum, or at least running down the people who had carried him away. Once at Brenton there was no difficulty in finding the Tyson home. It was a very fine mansion with big grounds about it, but Randy was not at all awed by that. He ran his machine up to the stone porch and ascending the steps rang the door bell. A servant answered the summons.

"Is Mr. Tyson at home?" Randy inquired.

"He is at home, yes," replied the servant, studying critically the dust-covered caller. "Business with him?"

"I have. You just tell him I am Randy Powell, from Seaside Park, and I came about the automobile accident."

The servant left Randy standing in the vestibule until a portly, consequential-looking man appeared. He viewed Randy in a shrewd, supercilious way.

"What's your business?" he challenged crisply.

"Are you Mr. Tyson?"

"Never mind that. What are you after?"

"But I do mind it," retorted Randy boldly. "If you are Mr. Tyson, it was your machine that ran down a friend of mine back at Seaside Park a couple of hours ago, and I want to know what you have done with him."

Mr. Tyson looked a trifle flustered; then very much annoyed. He said:

"I've done nothing with him. He just came along. Say, I hope you haven't gone and stirred up a lot of notoriety and trouble for me along the line."

"Why should I—unless you deserve it."

"Ha—hum!" muttered the millionaire. "See here, come in. You look reasonable—more so than that young wildcat friend of yours unless he has his own way."

Mr. Tyson led Randy into a magnificently furnished room, nodded him to a chair and sat down facing him.

"See here," he spoke, "you just tell me how much rumpus you have raised about this unfortunate affair."

"I've raised no rumpus," declared Randy. "I've simply run down your automobile, which the police of Seaside Park didn't seem able or inclined to do."

"I'm glad of that," said Mr. Tyson, apparently greatly relieved, "and there will be no trouble at all in fixing up things satisfactorily all around. You would have heard from me before midnight, for this Pep—ought to be called Pepper—just ordered that his friend at Seaside Park—I suppose it's you?"

"Yes, it's me," declared Randy.

"Well, he wanted word sent to you."

"Is he badly hurt?" inquired Randy solicitously.

"Not at all—but that isn't it. See here, lad, because I'm supposed to have a lot of money I seem to be a mark for everybody. I have been unfortunate enough to have various accidents with my machine. A month ago I ran down a man. About all he did was to stub his toe, but he's sued me for twenty thousand dollars damages and has a doctor ready to swear he is crippled for life. Last week I ran over a valuable dog at Seaside Park and the magistrate fined me fifty dollars for speeding over the limit, and said if there was another complaint he would give me a jail sentence. Ugh! fine thing to be rich; isn't it?"

Mr. Tyson really looked so disgusted that Randy could not refrain from smiling.

"The newspapers got hold of it and pictured me as a regular ogre. Now it wasn't our fault at all when this friend of yours got hurt this evening. He had no business in the street—don't you see?"

"Say, if he hadn't got there where would that child in the baby carriage be?" demanded Randy indignantly.

"Yes, that's true," agreed the millionaire slowly, "but even there they could not legally hold us. The baby carriage had no lights on it. Let all that go, though. This Pep was a brave fellow to risk his life for the child, and I'm glad he did it. My lawyer, after the last case, though, told me what to do in future accidents, so I followed his advice. I captured your friend and I intend to keep him captured."

"I don't think you will," began Randy, rising wrathfully to his feet. "He's a poor boy, but he's got some friends and——"

"Pish! Don't get excited. Keep cool, lad, hear me through. We rushed your friend here, summoned the best surgeon in Brenton, and this Pep of yours is snug and comfortable as a dormouse—in bed in the best room in the house.

I'm going to give him the best of care and pay him for any loss of time he may sustain. Isn't that fair?"

"Why—I suppose so," admitted Randy. "Only—what does Pep say?"

"Well, at first he was going to fight us, lame hand and all. Then the surgeon talked some sense into him, by telling him that if he would use a little care and not use his arm he would be well as ever inside of a week. If he didn't, he may have all kinds of complications in the future. To be frank with you, all I care for is to turn the boy out sound and well, so he can't be coming along later on with another of those twenty thousand dollar damage suits."

"Can I see him?" inquired Randy.

"You surely can," replied Mr. Tyson with alacrity, "and I hope you will coöperate with us in urging him to stay here and follow the directions of the doctor."

Mr. Tyson had not overstated the case when he told Randy that Pep was well cared for. As Randy entered a great luxuriously furnished room upstairs he saw his comrade propped up in bed, his arm in a sling and a table spread with dainties directly at hand.

"You tell him to stay here," whispered Mr. Tyson in Randy's ear, and left the two boys to themselves.

Pep grinned as he welcomed Randy. He moved his injured arm to show that he was by no means helpless.

"I'm booked here for a week, Randy," were his first words—"but why not? There won't be much to do around the new show for some days to come, and if there was I wouldn't be any help with my crippled arm."

Then Pep in a modest way went on to give details of the accident.

"You see," were his concluding remarks, "I'm comfortable and well cared for here and, as the surgeon says, I might have trouble with my arm if I got careless with it. Mr. Tyson says he will pay me for any loss time, so don't worry about me. I'll show up at Seaside Park before the week is over with a neat little lot of cash in my pocket, and fresh and strong to help get the new Wonderland in ship shape order."

Thus Pep dismissed the incident of the hour, so Randy went "home," rather lonesome without his chum. Neither guessed for a moment that there was to grow out of the circumstance something destined to affect their whole business career.

CHAPTER X—THE PRESS AGENT

"I hardly know how to thank you, Mr. Vincent," spoke Frank Durham.

"Don't try to," replied the ventriloquist, in his usual offhand way.

Frank, practically a beginner in the profession, and Hal Vincent, a seasoned graduate, were saying good-bye to each other on the steps of the building which contained the offices and warerooms of the great National Film Exchange.

For several days the ears of our young hero had buzzed with little besides "movies" chatter. When Frank had first gone into the business and had bid in at auction the outfit now at Fairlands, he had learned the basis of the trade through an interesting day spent at a motion picture supply house in the small city near his home. He found New York on a larger scale, however. Even within the few months that had elapsed since he and his chums had started the Wonderland photo playhouse there had been improvements, innovations and new wrinkles without number.

Frank now came in contact with these. It was a great advantage to him that he had Vincent to act as guide and adviser. The latter entered into the spirit of the occasion with the zest of an expert showing a novice the ground he has so often traversed. Vincent was not only active and obliging, but he was observant and shrewd. He knew the best supply sources in the city and how to handle them.

It embarrassed Frank the first time Vincent, in his breezy showman's way, introduced him to the proprietor of the National Film Exchange. According to the versatile and voluble ventriloquist, Frank and his chums, Randy and Pep, were young prodigies who had built up a mammoth photo playhouse enterprise at Fairlands out of nothing and had scored a phenomenal success. And still further, according to Vincent, Frank had secured a most favorable contract at Seaside Park, and was about to reap profits from a project that would set the pace in summer outing resorts for the season.

"Now this is confidential, Byllesby," observed Vincent, buttonholing the movies man and assuming a dreadfully important air, as he glanced mysteriously about the place as if fearful of eavesdroppers—"this is probably one of a chain of shows Durham may manage. Don't lisp it to anybody, but one of his backers is a lady—well, I think she is rated at a cool half-million in real coin. You won't have to wait for your money from the Durham combination, so hand out only the best and latest on the closest terms—understand?"

As said, Frank found that even within the six months that had passed since he had bought their original motion picture outfit science had been busy in the improvement of old and the invention of new devices. Kinetoscopes, cameragraphs—all the varied list of projecting apparatus had progressed fast. It kept his mind on the alert to catch the explanations of the newest thing in condensing glasses, front and rear; jackets and tubes, transformers, shutters, iris dissolvers, knife switches and slide carriers. It was all part of an education in the line of business activity he had adopted, however, and Frank drank in lots of knowledge during that New York trip.

He was full of pleasant anticipation and eager to rejoin his friends at Seaside Park, to go over with them his list of the wonderful things purchased and tell them about the satisfactory arrangements he had made for new feature films as they came along. He shook Vincent's hand heartily in parting. Frank added a word or two, telling how he hoped they would see the ventriloquist down at Seaside Park soon.

"I have a fair chance of getting something out of the road venture that burst up and left me stranded when I ran across Jolly," explained Vincent. "As soon as that is settled, which may be in less than a week, I'll be down at the new Wonderland—don't doubt it. Move on a bit; will you, Durham?" Vincent spoke in a quick undertone, his eyes fixed on an approaching pedestrian who at once attracted Frank's attention.

He was the typical tragedian out at elbows, but showing his consciousness of being "an actor." He wore one rusty glove. The other hand was thrust into the breast of his tightly buttoned frock coat. His hair was long, and his hat, once a silk tile, was dented and yellowed by usage. Frank's companion did not escape. The eagle eye of the oncomer was fixed upon him and would not leave him.

"Ah, Hal!" he hailed, extending his gloved hand with a bow of real elegance— "howdy. Off the circuit? So am I. I see you are eating," and he glanced up and down the new suit of clothes Vincent had been enabled to purchase from his share in the bird house speculation.

"That's about all I am able to arrange for," declared Vincent, bluntly.

"I expect a check," proceeded the newcomer grandly. "Avaricious, but wealthy relative. If I could anticipate till to-morrow, now——"

"Not from me, I can tell you that," interrupted Vincent definitely.

"Only a dollar. You see——"

"A dime wouldn't make any difference until I get my settlement from the people who sent me out to starve," insisted Vincent.

Frank was interested in the odd, airy individual, who struck him as a rather obsolete type of the fraternity. He smiled, and this was encouragement for the frayed actor, who touched his hat again and extended his gloved hand, this time towards Frank, with the words:

"Surely we have met somewhere on the boards? Was it in Philadelphia, when I was press agent for the United Thespian? Perhaps that will assist your memory."

Frank good-naturedly accepted and glanced over a very dirty and worn card bearing the inscription: "Roderick James Booth: Press Agent." Frank shook his head,

"I have not had the honor of meeting you before, Mr. Booth," he said.

"In the line, I suppose?" insinuated Booth.

"If you mean of theatricals—hardly," replied Frank. "I have done a little in the motion picture field."

"Ah!" exclaimed Booth, with great animation, striking a pose—"there, indeed, is a field. Young man; I proclaim a wonderful future for the photo playhouse. Let me see, where are you located now—and the name, I didn't quite catch the name?"

"I am Frank Durham," replied our young hero, "and with some others expect to open a new motion picture show at Seaside Park."

"Ah, a hit! Think of it! Beside the soothing waves, dancing breezes, vast throngs, stupendous profits. Only one thing lacking—an able press agent. Sir," and Booth raised himself to his loftiest height, "I papered Baltimore till the house was jammed. The United Thespians—sir, a moment, aside. Mr. Vincent will pardon us. Could you anticipate——"

Frank knew what was coming. The man did not look like a drinker and he did look hungry. Vincent nudged Frank warningly, but Frank could not resist a generous impulse.

Mr. Booth almost danced as a crisp dollar bill was placed in his hand. Then he took out a pencil and memorandum book. Very carefully and laboriously he began to write:

"Durham, Seaside Park. I. O. U. one dollar. Mem: suggest plan for publicity campaign."

"You've put your foot in it this time, Durham," exclaimed Vincent almost wrathfully, as with a great flourish Booth went on his way.

"Oh, pshaw!" laughed Frank, "the poor fellow probably needs a square meal."

"Yes, but you needn't have told him who you were and about the new Wonderland. Why, within an hour he will be telling his friends of a new opening at Seaside Park—engaged for the season—forfeit money already paid. Besides that, I wouldn't wonder to see him put in an appearance personally with one of his wild publicity schemes direct at Seaside Park. Oh, you can laugh, but once he sets out on your trail, and you encourage him, you'll find it no easy matter to shake him off," a prediction by the way that Frank and his chums had reason to recall a little later.

Frank was in fine spirits when he reached Seaside Park. Everything had gone famously with him in the city. He had been introduced to a man who operated a string of summer resort motion picture shows, and he had gleaned an immense amount of information. The man had reduced his special line to a science and had made money at it, and Frank was greatly encouraged.

It was late in the afternoon when he started from the depot for the new quarters. He was pleased and satisfied as his eye ran over the front of the old store. Various touches of paint had made the entrance attractive, the broad windows bore each a fine plain sign, and a very ornamental ticket booth was in place. Frank found the front doors partially open, and passed the length of the great room to come unawares upon his friends in the living quarters at the rear.

"Good!" shouted a familiar voice, and Ben Jolly, wearing a kitchen apron and just getting supper ready, waved a saucepan over his head in jubilant welcome.

"I say, you people have been doing some work here since I left," cried Frank, as he shook hands with Randy. "Why, where is Pep?"

"There's a story to that," explained Randy. "He's safe and sound, but may not be here till to-morrow or the next day."

"Gone home to see his folks?" hazarded Frank.

"No, not that," dissented Randy. "Tell you, Frank, it's quite a long story. Suppose we get the meal on the table, and seated comfortably, and we'll all have a lot to tell; eh?"

"Just the thing," voted Jolly with his usual enthusiasm. "I've got a famous rice pudding on the bill of fare, Durham, and I'll guarantee you'll enjoy a good home meal once more."

"That's just what I will," agreed Frank.

He sat down and busied himself sorting some bills and circulars with which his pockets were filled. Then, as the smoking viands were placed on the table, he joined his friends.

"Now then, Durham, you first," directed Jolly. "How's the New York end of the proposition?"

"Famous," reported Frank heartily. "I've made some fortunate discoveries and investments—pass the potatoes; will you, Randy?"

"Hold on!" cried a familiar voice—"I'm on the programme for some of that, too!"

CHAPTER XI—CROSSED WIRES

"Why, hello, Pep!" exclaimed Frank in joyful surprise, jumping up from the table and greeting the missing chum with a hearty handshake.

"Hold on—go a little easy on that hand," spoke the unexpected guest. "It's the one I hurt in that automobile accident, you know, and not quite as strong as it used to be."

"What automobile accident?" inquired Frank in surprise.

"Oh, that's so," broke in Randy quickly—"Frank has just got back from the city and hasn't heard of it yet. We didn't expect you so soon. You wrote us yesterday you wouldn't leave Brenton until Saturday."

"Humph! Had to," said Pep with a wry grimace.

"How is that?"

"Fired," explained Pep tersely, and looking as if he had not enjoyed the experience one bit. "Say, don't bother me now about it. I'm hungry as a bear, and had to walk eight miles to get here before dark, and I'll feel better natured when I've had something to eat and a little rest."

Ben Jolly arched his eyebrows in an inquiring way and Randy looked Pep over sharply. Jolly had just returned from Fairlands that morning, and Randy had heard from Pep by mail only twice during his sojourn at the Tyson home at Brenton. From all he had learned and seen during his brief visit there, Randy had been led to believe that Pep would return with waving colors. He would not only be mended up, as Randy had reason to figure it out, but would have a comfortable sum of money representing lost time.

Pep, however, did not look like a favorite of fortune. He used both hands with equal celerity in dispatching the meal, and his injured wrist seemed to give him no inconvenience or pain. His face was glum, however, and when he spoke of being "fired" Randy knew that something was up.

"Tell us about this accident of yours, Pep," urged Frank as all hands got over the first promptings of appetite.

"Randy will," snapped Pep.

Randy was agreeable to the suggestion. He was glad to descend on the heroism of his chum, and dwelt somewhat upon the bravery of Pep in risking his life for the little child in the baby carriage. Randy led the course of the narrative to his visit to Brenton, the peculiar situation in which he found Pep, and detailed the contents of the two letters he had received from their absent partner.

"Well, Pep," hailed Frank heartily, at the end of the story. "I suppose you've turned out an adopted son or great favorite with this Mr. Tyson."

Pep had just finished a second helping of Jolly's famous rice pudding and was ready to talk now.

"Oh, yes, I have! See me!" he retorted in a scornful and disgusted way. "Say, the next fellow who plays me for an invalid will be a good one, I tell you. It's all right up to where Randy left me in the arms of luxury at the Tyson residence. Yes, it was all right for two days after that. Then I got into my usual trim—restless. Of course I couldn't work with my bad arm, but it didn't bother me a bit. I told Mr. Tyson so. He spoke to that old fogy surgeon of his and after a regular battle we came to terms."

"What terms, Pep?" inquired Frank.

"I wanted something to do. I was dead sick of hanging around doing nothing. It seems that Mr. Tyson runs a broker's office in Brenton. It's a branch of a big Wall Street concern in New York City. They do some business, too, and he hires a lot of clerks. Well, the surgeon said that as long as I didn't use my bad arm it was all right, so old Tyson takes me down to the office. First day he put me at the information desk. Then the boy who held that position regularly came back and he set me at one of the telephones."

"What doing, Pep?" inquired Jolly.

"Taking quotations and orders on the long distance. The 'phone was arranged on a standard and I didn't have to handle it at all. I had a pad of paper at my side. All I had to do was to write out the quotations, or orders. Then I would touch an electric bell and a boy would take them to the manager."

"Sort of stock exchange business; eh?" propounded Jolly.

"Yes, that way," assented Pep. "The first day I got through grandly. Old Tyson told me I had the making of a smart man in me and advised me to cut away from the movies and become a second Vanderbilt. They kept me at the 'phone yesterday, too. It's too bad they did," added Pep grievously. "I reckon they think so now."

"Explain, Pep," urged the curious Randy.

"Well, about two o'clock in the afternoon there was a rush of business. Everybody in the office was busy. I heard the manager say that it looked like a regular Black Friday, whatever that was, the way stocks and bonds were being juggled. Right when everything was going at lightning speed and the office was in a turmoil, long distance says: 'Buy for Vandamann account at twenty'—and then there was a hiss and a jangle—crossed wires—see?"

Pep's engrossed auditors nodded silently, eager to hear the remainder of his story.

"Then I got the balance of the order—as I supposed—'one thousand shares Keystone Central.' Orders came piling up and I had all I could do to write them down. 'Buy one thousand Keystone Central at twenty' went to the manager with the rest. I thought no more of it until this morning. I was at my 'phone thinking of how I'd be home with the rest of you Saturday, when the manager, mad as a hornet, came to me. 'You see Mr. Tyson just as quick as you can,' he snapped at me, and I did. Mr. Tyson had just found out that I had mixed orders. I talked about crossed wire, but he wouldn't hear a word of it. 'The idea of loading us down with that bustling stock at twenty, when it was offered on the exchange at three cents yesterday!' he howled. 'Here get out of here and stay out of here. And here, you've cost a pretty penny, and you can take that stock for your pay.' And with that," concluded Pep, "he hurled this package at me, and I'm a bloated bondholder."

Pep drew a little package of green and yellow documents from his pocket. He flung them on the table in a disgruntled way. Ben Jolly picked them up and looked them over.

"Heard of the Keystone Central," he observed—"lot of watered stock and new people trying to squeeze out the old shareholders. Maybe a few dollars in these, Pep."

But the disgusted Pep waved documents and remark away with disdain.

"Burn 'em up; throw 'em away—don't care what you do with them," he declared. "I am sick of the whole business. I want to forget how mean money makes a millionaire, and just get back into the gladness and bustle of the old motion picture proposition."

"All right, Pep," said Jolly blandly, pocketing the papers. "I'll just take care of the documents for you. They may bob up in a new way some time; you never can tell."

"What about moving the outfit down from Fairlands, Mr. Jolly?" here interrupted Frank.

"That's so—my report is due; isn't it? Why, I've arranged for everything. Boxed up and crated what there was in good shape, and expect they'll arrive to-morrow or the next day."

"By rail, of course?"

"Oh, yes. It's a long distance, there's a lot of bad roads and hills to climb, and freight was the only way. I left the chairs. It would cost as much to move them as they were worth."

"We had better stock up new as to the seating feature," said Frank, "seeing that we need double what we had at Fairlands. Well, boys, now to show you what I have accomplished."

Frank had done so much that he held their fascinated attention unbroken for well nigh an hour. Jolly smiled and nodded his approval as Frank told in detail of his negotiations with the supply houses in the city. Pep's eyes snapped with anticipation of the brilliant way in which the new Wonderland was going to open.

"It looks all smooth sailing; doesn't it now?" Randy submitted in his optimistic way.

"How soon will we open?" pressed the eager Pep.

"I should think we would be all ready within a week or ten days."

"Oh, pshaw! have to wait that long?" mourned Pep.

"You want things right; don't you?" asked Randy.

"Oh, of course, of course," responded Pep, "only every day counts. Before we know it someone else will break in and get all the cream off the proposition."

"No, no, friend Pep," laughed Ben Jolly confidently. "We've got too good a start in the movies race at Seaside Park, and we're bound to win."

CHAPTER XII—BUSINESS RIVALS

"Put the brake on, Pep!" sang out Randy.

"What's the trouble now?" inquired Ben Jolly. "Someone trying to kidnap you again?"

Frank, Randy and Jolly, on their way to see about their goods at the freight house, had scattered precipitately as a bounding figure turned a street corner and almost crashed into them.

"Glad I found you. Say, what did I tell you?" exclaimed the youthful sprinter. "You come with me and I'll show you something that will open your eyes."

"Later, Pep," said Frank. "We are on our way to arrange for carting the traps from Fairlands up to the playhouse."

"It won't take a minute," declared Pep. "It's only a block or two away. Say, you'd better come. I'll show you a sight that will set you thinking."

"All right, we'll give you five minutes, Pep," said Frank indulgently.

"And don't forget that I told you so!"

"Told us what?" interrogated Randy.

"You'll find out in a minute."

Pep piloted the group in his usual impetuous way. Quite a busy boardwalk diverged from the main boardwalk thoroughfare, and some minor stores and restaurants of the cheaper class occupied the first block.

About midway of the square was a vacant building, once a dime museum. Frank and his friends had noticed this in their search for a business location. It was off the main route of travel, however, and the building was old, ramshackly and set down from the street level, the lot lying in a depression in the ground so that one had to descend three steps to the entrance.

"There you are," pronounced Pep in an impressive way. "What do you say to it?"

Frank, Randy and Ben Jolly came to a halt as they faced an electric sign running out from the front of the building.

"'National,'" read Randy—"'National' what?"

"Photo playhouse," asserted Pep.

"Do you know that?" challenged Jolly.

"I do. When I passed by a man who was wiring the sign told me that a big New York fellow and a Seaside Park party were going to open up next week."

"The mischief!" exclaimed Randy, roused up.

"Say," remarked Jolly, bristling up at this hint of rivalry, "we want to get busy."

"Oh, it doesn't alarm me," spoke Frank. "In the first place it is off the mainly traveled route. Besides, the neighborhood is cheap and I would imagine they wouldn't get more than a nickel."

"It's worth looking up—always keep track of what your competitors are doing," advised Jolly.

"Why I say," suddenly remarked Frank—"their sign is wrong."

"How wrong?" questioned Randy, and then he added: "That's so: 'NATONAL.' They've left out an I."

"It's so," cried Pep, "maybe they bought some second hand letters and there wasn't any I's in the lot."

"Big New York fellow,'" observed Jolly thoughtfully. "Wonder who he is? Maybe you stirred things up in the city, Durham, and started somebody on our trail."

"Well, we must expect competition," replied Frank. "It shan't scare us."

"No, we'll stick to a first-class basis and be the leader," declared Randy.

"You fellows go on," spoke Pep. "I'll sort of spy out the enemy's country— hey?"

"I would like to know who is behind this 'National' with an I missing," said Frank, and they turned about and resumed their way to the freight depot, leaving Pep to his own devices.

Pep was not afraid to venture anywhere or address anybody. He was inside the old building and had accosted the man he had seen outside within five minutes after his friends left him. The man knew all about the proposed extensive refitting of the old barn of a place, but did not know who was backing the new show outside of a big man from New York and a party with money at Seaside Park. Pep pumped him dry so far as the arrangements for the show were concerned.

"Hello, Pep," hailed him just as he went outside again.

"That isn't my name—it's Pepperill," retorted Pep, resenting the mistake and the familiarity. He was in a fiery mood just now, but as he recognized young Peter Carrington and noticed that he was headed for the building he had just left, Pep decided that he would lose nothing by using a little tact.

"Well, that's all right," observed Peter in his usual airy manner—"been into my show?"

"Your show?"

"That's what," and Peter poked his cap back on his head, stuck his thumbs in his armpits, and grinned at Pep in a patronizing sort of way.

"Oh, I see," said Pep, "you're the Seaside Park capitalist I heard about?"

"Did some one honest say that?" inquired Peter, his vanity immensely gratified. "Well, I have invested something—got a little money from my aunt, although she doesn't know that I've gone into the show business. She'd be mad if she knew I was going to set up opposition to you fellows, for she likes you. Business is business, though. You fellows wouldn't take me in and I had to get some other partners; didn't I?"

"Who are your partners?" probed Pep innocently.

"Well, one of them is Greg Grayson. He's from your town. You know him?"

"Slightly," assented Pep, his lips drawing together grimly.

"A friend of his has invested something, too," rambled on the effusive Peter. "Our mainstay, though, is a New York man. They say he's 'way up in the moving picture line."

"What is his name?" pressed Pep.

"Mr. John Beavers—ever hear of him?"

"I don't think I have."

"That's because you're new in the business," declared Peter. "He says he's the first man who ever started a moving picture show."

"Also a capitalist, I suppose?" insinuated Pep.

"Well, he's got a lot of investments that have tied up his ready cash, he says, but he will stand back of us if we need more money."

"Well," said Pep, "I must be moving on. The more the merrier, you know."

"I must tell you," hurried on Peter—"We're going to have two private boxes in our show."

"What for?"

"Oh, to make a hit. Friends, members of the press and all that—see? I say, Smith, I hope you're going to exchange professional courtesies."

"What do you mean?" demanded Pep.

"Complimentaries, and all that."

"I don't think we are going to have any complimentaries," replied Pep. "Our space will be for sale; not to give away. That fellow run a photo playhouse!" snorted Pep wrath fully to himself, as he left the spot. "Why, he hasn't got the gumption to run a peddler's cart, or a shoestring stand!"

Pep reached the freight house just as his friends were leaving it. They had arranged for the reception and delivery of their traps from Fairlands to the new playhouse. This meant busy times, getting in order to open up for business. Pep told of his new discoveries as to the personnel of the rival firm of the "Natonal." Randy flared up at once.

"It's half spite work," he declared. "This Peter is mad because we wouldn't take him into our scheme and Greg Grayson owes us a grudge, or fancies he does, and wants to pay it back. He and his cronies were always ready for any mean mischief back at Fairlands."

"Oh, well, as long as it is fair business rivalry, who cares?" submitted Jolly. "From the start they've made I don't think they will last long."

"They will do all they can to annoy us while they do," declared Pep.

"Did you tell young Carrington about the missing letter in the 'Natonal' sign, Pep?" inquired Frank.

"No, I didn't," replied Pep, ungraciously. "Think I'm around mending his blunders? Humph! guess not. If I had, do you know what he would have said?"

"No; what, Pep?" pressed Randy, with a broad grin.

"He'd say: 'Oh, yes, that's so. Anybody can see it's spelled wrong. Didn't notice it before. Of course it should be "Natonel.""

All hands laughed at Pep's sally. Then Frank asked:

"Did you ever hear of this John Beavers, Mr. Jolly?"

"Never did, Durham. I wonder where the crowd picked him up? Don't think he's a notable, though. Judging from the way he's letting them hold the bag, I reckon he isn't much of a capitalist."

They emerged upon the boardwalk as Jolly concluded his remarks. Pep was the first to discover a commotion amid the crowds ahead.

"There's some new excitement," he cried. "Let's hurry up and see what it is."

Just then a man dashed through the throng on a dead run. In hot pursuit was a second individual, fast overtaking him and shouting as he sprinted:

"Stop that man!"

CHAPTER XIII—ALL READY!

The man in advance happened to cross a wet streak on the walk just as Frank and his friends observed him. This was caused by the overflow of a combination drinking fountain and horse trough. The man slipped and went flat. In another minute, as he struggled to his feet, his pursuer pounced upon him.

"Why, look! Look!" ejaculated Pep.

"It's Hal!" echoed Ben Jolly.

Frank and Randy recognized their friend the ventriloquist simultaneously. The former was a good deal surprised, for he had bade Vincent good-bye in New York City within the past forty-eight hours. He wondered what had brought Vincent to Seaside Park; and more than ever, what his participation in the present incident might mean.

"I've got you; have I?" stormed Vincent, making a grab at the fugitive and seizing him by the arm. Then he whirled him around and transferred his clutch to the throat of the man. "Now, then, you pull off that coat in a jiffy, or I'll fling you out into the street."

"Yes, yes, certainly—ssh! don't raise a row. Likely to be known here. Going into business—hurt my reputation."

"Your reputation, you miserable rat!" shouted Vincent, greatly excited. "You've led me a fine chase; haven't you, after all I did for you! I made up my mind, though, I'd find you and get back my property, if I had to chase you half over the country."

"Return coat in private—secluded spot."

"Take it off now!"

"Leaves me without any."

"Take it off!" fairly yelled Vincent. Then, as the man obeyed he wrenched it from his grasp, threw it to the pavement and grasping the fugitive by the shoulders, ran him straight up to the watering trough.

Splash! splash! splash! "Ooo—oof! Leggo! Murder!"—a wild riot of sounds made the welkin ring. A fast-gathering mob bustled nearer. Dripping, hatless, coatless, the helpless fugitive was given a shove down the sidewalk by Vincent, who turned and confronted a police officer.

"Hi, there!" challenged the latter sternly—"what's the trouble here?"

"No trouble at all," retorted Vincent. "I've saved you that. That fellow slinking out of sight between those two buildings stole my coat and I've got it back—that's all."

"A thief; eh?"

"Oh, he's out of sight and I'm satisfied," advised Vincent. "I gave him free lodging and feed in the city and he paid me back by robbing me. We're square now and no need of your services, thank you. By the way, though, you might glimpse him so as to be able to keep track of him. He's a slippery customer to have in a town where there's even door mats or lawn mowers lying around loose."

Frank had picked up the coat from the pavement where Vincent had flung it and he now offered it to him.

"That you, Durham?" hailed the ventriloquist, mopping his perspiring brow—"and the rest of the crowd? Howdy—I declare, I was ruffled. I can stand anything but ingratitude."

"Who is the fellow, anyway?" inquired Jolly.

"Oh, he's been a hanger-on at the movies and a sponge and dead beat for a long time. His name is Jack Beavers."

"What's that?" cried Pep, sharply. "Why, that's the name of the 'big New York man' who is going to start the new show with Peter Carrington and his crowd."

"What new show?" inquired Vincent, quickly.

Pep told of the prospective photo playhouse that had come to their attention that day.

"Say," exclaimed Vincent, belligerently, when the information had been accorded. "I'll follow this up and put that fellow out of business."

"I wouldn't trouble, Mr. Vincent," said Frank. "We don't want to give Carrington and his friends any excuse for claiming we are persecuting them. If this man is the kind of fellow you describe, he will soon run himself out."

"And them, too," declared Jolly.

"Birds of a feather—all of them," commented Pep.

Vincent explained that he was due to return at once to the city. He expected to have his claim against the company that had stranded him and owed him money come up in court at any time, and wanted to be on hand to present his evidence. The boys, however, prevailed upon him to accompany them home and have at least one good, old-fashioned meal with them. Then they all went with him to his train.

"Hope to see you soon again, Hal," remarked Ben Jolly, as they shook hands good-bye.

"You will, Jolly—it's fate," declared Vincent. "I'm running up against your crowd all the time, and I guess it's on the books. Bow-wow-wow!" and he winked at Pep, always alive for mischief.

"Meow!—p'st! pst!"—and a kitten in the arms of a fussy old man just getting aboard of a coach arched its back at the well-counterfeited imitation of the ventriloquist, while its mistress ran up the steps in a violent flurry.

"Let me out—let me out!" came next, apparently from a big sample case a colored porter was carrying for a traveling salesman. Down came the case with a slam and the porter stood regarding it with distended eyes and quivering face.

"Lawsy sakes, boss!" he gurgled—"what you done got in dere?" and very gingerly and rapidly he carried the case into the coach when prevailed upon to do so by its somewhat startled owner.

Then with a smile the versatile Vincent jumped aboard of the train, waving his hand cheerily in adieu to his smiling friends.

"A jolly good fellow, that," commented Frank, as the train pulled out. "I only hope we will be able to afford to engage his talents for the new Wonderland."

"You've just got to," vociferated Pep. "He's a regular drawing card and a show all in himself."

And now came the real work of the motion picture chums. The new photo playhouse was all ready for the outfit, and when that was brought from the freight house there was plenty of lifting, carrying and placing to attend to. The big electric sign had to be reset and adjusted, the sheet iron booth for the machine put in place, and for four days there were a multitude of little things to accomplish.

Jolly got track of a closed show at Brenton where the chairs were for sale and drove an excellent bargain in their purchase, and also in the delivery.

It was Thursday night when for the first time the electric lights were turned on, so the boys could see how the playhouse "showed up," as they expressed it. They all went out in front, Jolly turning the switches from inside. To the excited vision of the enthusiastic Pep the result was a burst of glory. The sign came out boldly. The many windows of the building, standing alone by itself as it did, made Randy think of a palace.

Frank was more than pleased. He was proud of his playhouse, proud of his loyal friends and deeply gratified as a crowd began to gather and he overheard their flattering and encouraging comments.

"Why, I saw that blaze three blocks down the street," declared a breathless urchin, coming up on a run.

"Yes, it was so bright I thought it was a fire," echoed a companion.

It was arranged that the three chums should visit their home town next morning. Jolly was left in charge of the playhouse and told them to have a good time and throw all care from their minds, as he would be able to complete all the arrangements for the opening Monday night.

The boys had a splendid time at Fairlands. They were highly elated over their business progress in the new venture and infused their families and friends with their own enthusiasm and delight. The Fairlands weekly paper printed a nice article about "Three Rising Young Business Men of Our Town," and altogether as they took the train to return to Seaside Park each one of the trio felt that life was worth living and honorable business success a boon well worth striving for.

"And now for the grandest event of our life," announced Pep, buoyantly— "the Opening Night!"

CHAPTER XIV—"THE GREAT UNKNOWN"

Pep Smith was up before the birds that memorable opening day. Pep had gone through a like experience when the Wonderland motion picture show was started at his home town, but that was a small proposition compared to the present one. To Pep's way of thinking the world was waiting for the great event. In his active mind he pictured eager hundreds counting the slow hours of the day until the first films were flashed upon the screen of the new photo playhouse.

Pep bustled about, broke into whistling and stirred things up so generally that he finally woke Ben Jolly. The latter was quite as interested as Pep in the doings of the day, only he concealed the true state of his feelings. He set about making preparations for breakfast as an excuse for rousing Frank and Randy.

"Well, Pep, this is the big day of our lives; eh?" propounded the good-natured cook, while his accommodating assistant was setting the table.

"And the finest ever seen," replied Pep. "I never saw such a daybreak. It's going to be just warm enough to make people want to stay out for the evening breeze, and that means crowds passing our place until late."

It was a jolly quartette that sat down at the table about five o'clock. The rest over Sunday had done them all good. No details had been left to chance or haste. Much satisfaction was felt in the knowledge that all the work thus far had been done well, with no loose ends to bother about when the programme began.

"There's some song posters to put up—they are due in the morning mail," observed Randy.

"Yes, and if that new film winder is sent along we might install it in place of the old one we brought from Fairlands," suggested Jolly. "I suppose you want to go through a test before night, Durham?"

"So as to give you the music cues? I think we had better," assented Frank. "Besides, we had better see that the films run smooth."

"I sent for a piano-tuning key to the city Saturday," said Jolly. "As soon as I get it I will give the instrument a little overhauling. Jolting over one hundred miles in a freight car doesn't improve the tone any."

Randy and Pep went out together about ten o'clock to get some posters from the printers. Frank had brought from the city quite a lot of gaily colored sheets with a blank space left at the top. Here the name and location of the new playhouse had been inserted. It took the boys until noon to get these placed. They posted them in nearly all the stores along the boardwalk. The hotel they had stayed at let them put two in the lobby, and they covered the town in a way satisfactory to themselves.

"Wonder what the National people are thinking of doing?" submitted Randy, as they sat down to dinner.

"They are going to open to-night—that's one thing I know," reported Pep.

"They're not making much stir about it, then," observed Jolly. "I haven't heard anybody speak about it, whom I ran across to-day."

"I met the man who is doing their electrical work," said Pep. "He and I are quite chummy. He told me they were in a fearful mix-up, with things half provided for, but that they would surely open this evening."

"What's it to be—a nickel?" inquired Jolly.

"No a dime, he says; but he showed me a bunch of complimentaries and laughed and said he'd sell them cheap. I haven't set my eyes on that Peter and the fellow from Fairlands anywhere around town, but I guess they're pitching in with the workman to get things in order."

Wednesday of the week previous a neat postal card telling of the new photo playhouse had been sent out to every name in the little local directory of Seaside Park. The hotel men had taken a bunch of these and had agreed to put one in the mail of each guest. The local paper happened to be an exchange of the Fairlands weekly, and the editor of the latter had given Frank a letter of introduction to the Seaside Park publisher. As a result, the latter had copied the article about the chums from the home paper and had also given a glowing description of the new playhouse on the beach.

It was about two o'clock in the afternoon when the lively Pep came into the playhouse with a new excitement on his mind.

"Say, fellows," he announced, "we're clear beat out."

"Hi! what's up now?" asked Ben Jolly.

"The National without an I has got us going. Just met Peter Carrington. He's jumping around like a chicken on a hot griddle. Just had time to flash by me and crow out, 'Watch out for our grand free concert to-night.'"

"Is that so—hum!" observed Jolly, musingly. "I wish I'd thought of that. I suppose we ought to make some little noise the opening night. Too late to arrange for it now, though. Just in time for practice, Pep. Put on that best coat of yours and a flower in your buttonhole, and usher in imaginary thousands, while Powell piles up uncounted dimes in the ticket office and Durham shoots the films. Ready—go!" and with a crash of the piano keys the volatile fellow began a lively overture.

"A small but critical audience pronounced the rehearsal A..," declared Jolly with a thrilling sweep of the piano keys as the three films were reeled off from the operator's booth. "Slow on that last picture, though, Durham. It's a good one and any audience will be glad to see it prolonged."

"Yes, being an ocean scene, I should think 'A Wrecker's Romance' would take great with the smell of real salt water blowing right into the playhouse," submitted Randy.

"Where the old wrecker hails the ship in the fog I want to work in some slow, solemn music," proceeded Jolly. "Eh? What's that? Mr. Jolly? That's me. What is it, lad?"

A messenger boy from the hotel had appeared at the entrance to the playhouse and asked for Mr. Benjamin Jolly. He delivered a note to that individual. The latter read it, his face breaking into a delighted smile.

"Say, my friends," he announced, seizing his hat and rushing unceremoniously from their company, "rush call, important though unexpected. Back soon," and Jolly chuckled and waved his hand gaily.

He was all smiles and still chuckling when he returned, which was in about an hour. They had decided on an early supper so as to have plenty of leisure to look over things before the playhouse opened, at half past six o'clock. As a starter, they planned to give three entertainments, each beginning on the hour.

"You seem to feel pretty good, Mr. Jolly?" observed Randy, as they dispatched the appetizing meal, their helpful friend brimming over with comical sayings.

"Oh, I've got to live up to my name, you know," explained Jolly. "Besides, always dreaming, you see. Been dreaming this afternoon of big houses, delighted throngs, pleasant surprises," and the speaker emphasized the last word, looking mysterious the while.

Frank and Randy, full of the theme of the hour and its practical demands upon their abilities, did not notice this particularly. Pep, however, eyed Jolly keenly. He lingered as his chums got up from the table. Somehow the exaggerated jollity of their lively pianist, to Pep's way of thinking, was connected with the mysterious message he had received earlier in the afternoon. Pep was an unusually observant lad. He was furthermore given to indulging a very lively fancy.

Now he went up to Jolly. Very searchingly he fixed his eye upon the piano player. Very solemnly he picked up one of Jolly's hands and looked up the arm of his coat.

"Hello!" challenged Jolly—"what you up to now, you young skeesicks?"

"Oh, nothing," retorted Pep—"just thought I'd like to see what you've got up your sleeve, as the saying goes."

"Ah," smiled Jolly—"suspect something; do you?"

"Got a right to; haven't I?" questioned Pep, shrewdly.

"Well," retorted Jolly, slowly, stroking his chin in a reflective way, "I won't say—just now. I'll give you a tip, though, Pep."

"Yes?" cried Pep, expectantly.

"About six-thirty look out for something."

"What will it be, now?" projected Pep, eagerly.

"The Great Unknown," replied Ben Jolly, with an enigmatical smile.

CHAPTER XV—THE SPEAKING PICTURE

Pep was "on pins and needles" over the mysterious remark of Ben Jolly as to "The Great Unknown." His friend was good natured about the matter, but parried all further questions. Then all hands at the new Wonderland became absorbed in their respective duties as partners and helpers in making the opening night of their venture a pronounced success.

Randy could not resist the temptation of taking a run past the National. He came back with his face on a broad grin.

"Well, Randy?" spoke Frank, expectantly.

"Carrington and his crowd are all business," was the report. "I could see Greg and another bustling about inside. Everything looks make-shift, though, as if they had rushed things and weren't more than half ready to begin. They were setting bare boards on top of kegs to answer for seats, and they had mended one of their broken front windows with a piece of canvas."

"Did you see anything of the famous band we heard about?" inquired Frank.

"No, but at one side of the steps that lead into the National there was a little platform with four chairs on it."

"I think that is their stand for the free concert Peter Carrington was bragging about," remarked Jolly.

"Four, did you say?" queried Pep, quickly. "Why, say, I'll bet I know."

"Know what, Pep?" inquired Jolly.

"About their band. Bet you it's those four fellows who wander around calling themselves the Little German Band. They play for lunches, or take up a collection from the crowd, most any way to pick up a few pennies. And, oh, such music! I heard them down at the merry-go-round yesterday."

"And that isn't all," added Randy. "Somewhere they have bought an old transparency. Strung it clear across the front of the building. It reads in big red letters, 'Grand Opening.' That's all right at a distance, but as you get nearer up to it you can see where the color has faded where they tried to paint out a smaller line. 'Free Lunch All Day' was the line I made out plain as could be. You can imagine where it came from."

Pep kept his watch in his hand and his eyes fixed upon it most of the time for the next half-hour. He almost counted the seconds in his impatience to see operations begin. He strolled restlessly between the living room where his friends sat conversing, to the front of the place, peering out of the windows and reporting progress at each trip:

"Lot of people looking over the place.

"Quite a crowd strolling by as if hanging around just waiting to get into the show.

"Dozen children in line waiting to buy tickets.

"Looks to me as if the people are heading from the beach in this direction. Hope we'll be able to handle the crowds.

"Say, Frank, it's twenty minutes after six."

"The crowds will keep, Pep," said Frank with a smile. "We've got to follow up a system, you know."

"For mercy's sake, what is that!" shouted Randy, suddenly.

There had swept in through the open windows upon the evening breeze a strange—a startling—series of sounds: "Ump! Ump!" "Bla-aat bla-aat," "Flar-op, flar-op," "Tootle-tootle"—a dismal melody filled the room, half notes, a mixture of notes, some of sledge hammer force, some weak and squeaking.

"Oh, hold me!" cried Randy, going into convulsions of laughter—"it's that Little German Band."

This seemed true, for they could trace the source of the music after a moment or two. They proceeded from the neighborhood of their business rival. How they might sound directly at their source it was difficult to surmise. Arising from the hollow in which the National was located, they lacked all acoustic qualities, like a band playing into a funnel.

"Twenty-seven minutes and a half after six," declared Pep abruptly.

"All right," nodded Jolly, arising from his seat. "It's not dark yet, but I suppose we will have to shoot on the lights."

The quartette started from the rear room in company, but Pep was making for the front entrance as soon as Jolly moved towards the piano. He came to a dead halt with a blank face as there sounded out, directly in front of the place, a sharp, clear bugle call.

"Ahem!" observed Ben Jolly, with significant emphasis.

Frank and Randy stood stock still. They were both surprised and entranced, for after that rollicking bugle call there rang out a sweet home melody. Whoever was creating those gentle yet clear and expressive notes was a master of the cornet. The hour, the scene were in harmony with the liquid notes that gushed forth like golden beads dropped into a crystal dish.

The wondering Pep, as if in a spell, moved noiselessly down the aisle and looked out through a window. Standing at the extreme inner edge of the walk was the cornetist. He wore a neat military costume. His close bearded face made Pep think of photographs he had seen of the leader of a noted military band. From every direction the crowds were gathering. They blocked the walk and the beach beyond it. A hush showed the appreciation of this enchanted audience until the tune was finished. Then the air was filled with acclamations.

"Friend of mine—it's all right. Thought I'd sort of offset that brass band down at the National," sang out Ben Jolly at the piano, and Pep now knew what his reticent friend had "up his sleeve." "All ready—here she goes!"

A chorus of "Ah's!" and "Oh's!" swelled forth as the electric sign and then the whole front of Wonderland burst into a glow of electric radiance. Frank was into the sheet iron booth in a jiffy. Jolly sat prim and precise at the piano. Randy was in place in the little ticket office just as Pep threw open the front doors.

Pep tried to look and act dignified, and did very well, but he felt so elated as the crowd poured in that he was all smiles and made everybody feel at ease instead of awed. Wonderland could not have opened at a more favorable moment. A better advertisement than the cornet solo could not have been devised. The crowd attracted by the music lingered, and most of them decided to take in the show.

Nearly every seat in the house was taken as Jolly began the overture. As the electric bell announced the darkening of the room Pep had to hunt for vacant chairs.

Pep was particularly attentive to the cornetist, who entered the playhouse after giving a second tune on his instrument.

"Near the front, please," he said to Pep, and he seemed satisfied as the young usher found him a chair in the front row next to the curtain.

The first film was full of fun and laughter. The second was an airship specialty and went off very well. The feature film of the series was "A Wrecker's Romance." It had just enough sea flavor to catch with the audience. There was a schooner caught in a storm that was lost in the gathering fog after sending up a rocket as a signal of distress.

The next scene showed the wrecker on the rainswept beach staring into the depths for some sign from the belated ship. It was here that Ben Jolly adapted the slow, striking music to the progress of the story.

Suddenly the lone figure on the beach lifted his hands to his lips, formed into a human speaking trumpet.

The audience, rapt with the intensity of the incident, were breathlessly engrossed. They could anticipate his forlorn call amid that desolate scene.

And then something remarkable happened. Apparently from those moving lips, distant but clear—resonant and long-drawn-out—thrilling every soul in the audience with its naturalness and intensity, there sounded the words:

"Ship ahoy!"

CHAPTER XVI—A GRAND SUCCESS

A deep hush pervaded the audience. The people were spellbound. Even Pep, standing against the side wall, felt a thrill pass through him. So natural and fitting had been the climax of the picture that its effect was apparent in a general rustling—a deep breath that swayed the onlookers.

The wrecker turned and his lips again moved as if to form for a signal whistle. Shrilly the call wavered about the scene.

"A talking picture!" Pep heard someone whisper.

"It's great!" echoed another voice.

A magnificent Newfoundland dog came bounding down the beach. Its young master held a coil of rope in his hand. He seemed swayed by conflicting emotions. Then he appeared to arrive at a conclusion.

He would not see that noble ship go to pieces on the rocks! He secured one end of the rope to the collar of the animal and made signs. The intelligent dog lifted his head. A joyous, willing bark rang out. It was real—like the call—like the whistle.

"Ginger!" exclaimed Pep Smith, in a stupefied way.

The dog disappeared. Then a dim light showed far out at sea and there sounded out the distant echo of the foghorn of a steamer. It was so familiar to the audience, so natural, that more than one among them probably lost himself and almost fancied he was standing on that lonely storm-lashed beach with the wrecker.

The film ran its course—the rope was carried by the faithful dog to the imperiled ship. A safety line was sent ashore. Passengers and crew were all saved and among them a beautiful young girl.

The last picture showed a lovely garden—the grounds of the home of the father of the rescued girl. She was reading a book in a vernal bower. The wrecker, her lover, appeared. Birds swayed among the blossoming branches of the trees. He spoke—she listened. Then, arm in arm, they walked slowly from the garden to the accompaniment of soft bird notes that filled the whole house with the most ravishing melody.

The lights came on amid furious and genuine applause. A delighted and excited old man jumped up on his chair and waved his hat, shouting:

"Three cheers for the best show on earth!"

"That was just famous."

"Must be one of those new speaking pictures."

"Oh, we must get all the folks to come to this delightful show!"

Pep's heart beat proudly as the audience filed out and he overheard this encouraging praise. He could hardly contain himself. Then he noticed Ben Jolly beckoning to him and he glided over to the piano. Jolly's face was one broad, delighted smile.

"How was it, Pep?" he inquired.

"No, what was it!" corrected Pep in a fluster, and then he noticed that the cornetist had remained seated—and he guessed something.

"Him?" he questioned.

"Correct!" replied Jolly. "Give Durham the tip. It's Hal Vincent. Durham must have noticed the brilliant accompaniment to the films and I don't want to get him rattled wondering what's up."

Pep had some difficulty in getting to the operator's booth. A long line of people were in place at the doors and they came in with a rush as the room was emptied. Pep tapped and Frank told him to come in.

"Did you hear—did you notice it?" spoke Pep, excitedly.

"Why, of course," replied Frank. "I couldn't understand it at first, but I know it must be some professional imitator."

"It was Mr. Vincent. He wore a false beard."

"You don't say so!" cried Frank.

"Yes, and he was the cornetist outside, too." Pep went on.

"All a piece of Mr. Jolly's work, I suppose?"

"Of course," replied Pep. "When he got that message this afternoon Mr. Vincent was probably at the hotel. Then he arranged to surprise us."

"It's more than a surprise—it's given tone and novelty to the whole entertainment."

The routine of set duties prevented the boys from prolonging the conversation. Jolly had begun the intermission overture and the seats were filling up fast. A good many had remained from the first audience. It took little circulating among the benches for Pep to learn that "A Wrecker's Romance," with its realistic interpretation, was responsible for this.

There was not a break in the second show, but there was a great surprise for the boys when the third and last programme began. A good many who had been to the National had got around to the rival playhouse. Home-going crowds from the beach made a stop.

"Nearly fifty people turned away," reported Randy, as Pep slipped out to have a word with him.

"There must have been over eight hundred admissions," figured Pep.

"One thousand, one hundred and fifty exactly," reported Randy.

"Why, say," cried Pep, "at that rate we're going to be rich!"

"Hey, young fellow," hailed a man appearing at this moment—"I suppose there's a free list for friends?"

"I should say so," responded Pep, recognizing the workman at the National he had gotten so chummy with. "Step right in, although I'm afraid I can't offer you a seat."

"Crowded as that; eh?" spoke the man. "That's fine."

"How is it at the National?" asked Pep. "Do they keep busy?"

"Every seat taken, but then you know they gave away a lot of tickets. Why, say," proceeded the man as they got inside, "I had no idea you could fix this place up so nifty."

"I suppose they opened at the National before they were all ready?" suggested Pep, who was dreadfully curious about the proceedings of Peter Carrington and his friends.

"I should say they did! They had to use boards for seats and several of them split in two. The funniest thing, though, was when one of the private boxes broke down."

"Say," propounded Pep, "did they really build some private boxes?"

"They did, for a fact. They were no use and no ornament, and the fellow who bosses things—his name is Beavers—kicked big against it. Young Carrington would have it, though, so we hurried through the best we could to-day. We told him the floor wasn't in and not to move the chairs about, but he got in there with some chums. First thing we knew one of them shifted his position, and the three of them went through the floor and landed sprawling on top of the piano. It was a sight, I tell you, and the audience roared."

"Well, I declare!" spoke Jolly, an hour later, as he came to the front of the playhouse with Vincent. "The last entertainment over and I believe you could gather up enough to run another show."

"It certainly looks like it," added Frank.

The last audience had dispersed, but around and near the Wonderland a great many persons and groups loitered or strolled along leisurely. They were the late stayers about the beach, and had the lights been left on and the ticket office open many of them no doubt would have entered the playhouse.

"Enough is as good as a feast," laughed Randy, hugging his tin cash box under his arm with great complacency. "It couldn't have been better."

"I guess we've hit it this time," pronounced Pep, proudly.

"That isn't always so hard to do at the start," advised Hal Vincent. "It's keeping it up that counts. You want to advertise now—new stunts, novelties, attractions."

"Attractions!" cried Pep. "Can the best of them beat those cornet solos? Novelties! Why, those talking pictures will be the hit of the town."

"You are a famous friend, Mr. Vincent," spoke Frank, warmly.

"And ought to be a famous man," supplemented Jolly, loyally. "He's worth putting on a special programme, Durham."

"I got through with my city lawsuit just in time," explained Vincent. "Made quite a good settlement, too. First thing I did was to release my wardrobe and dummies from embargo. They are ready to ship to any point where I may find an engagement."

"Then give your order for their delivery at Seaside Park forthwith, Mr. Vincent," directed Frank, spontaneously. "I'll risk saying that we can pay you what is fair for a month's steady run at least."

"Things seem to be building up right along the line; don't they, Pep?" piped the piano player briskly, giving his favorite a friendly slap on the shoulder.

"Oh!" cried Randy, "we're going to find all kinds of fame and fortune at Seaside Park."

"By—the—wild—sea—waaa-ves!" added the versatile Vincent, throwing his ventriloquist voice way off over the beach in a sing-song way that startled passers-by.

CHAPTER XVII—BOASTFUL PETER

"Somebody at the door, Pep."

"All right, I'll attend to them."

Jolly was rearranging the chairs after sweeping out the playhouse and Pep was dusting, when there came a summons at the front door. It was a smart tapping and Pep wondered who it could be. He released one door to confront an impressive-looking individual, with a light cane in his hand and a face that somehow made Pep think of a stranded actor.

"This is the Wonderland, I assume?" spoke the caller, grandiloquently.

"You have assumed right," replied Pep.

"Mr. Frank Durham, proprietor?"

"One of them."

"Can I see Mr. Durham personally. Important business."

"Certainly. This way," directed Pep, and he led the way to the living room at the rear.

"What did I tell you!" half groaned Hal Vincent into Frank's ear the moment he set eyes on the newcomer.

"Ah, Mr. Durham—forgotten me, I suppose?" airily intimated the visitor, as he entered the room.

"Not at all," replied Frank, with a pleasant smile, as he arose from the desk at which he was seated.

Jolly had got hold of a very presentable desk in his trading. It had been set in a convenient corner of the room and constituted the "office" of the Wonderland.

It was the ubiquitous Booth whom Frank greeted. He knew the man at a glance and so did Vincent. The latter viewed the new arrival suspiciously and with a none too cordial bow. There was something that appealed to Frank in the visionary old fellow, however, and he treated him courteously.

Booth bore unmistakable signs of prosperity and contentment. He now wore a brand new glossy silk tile, lemon colored gloves, was cleanly shaven and exploited an irreproachable collar and bright red necktie. He might have been one of the amusement kings of America judging from the immense gravity and dignity of his demeanor. Mr. Booth drew out a memorandum book with several bank notes folded between its pages and straightened his neat gold eyeglasses.

"I have some very pretentious business offerings for you, Mr. Durham," he volunteered. "However, before we proceed any farther, there is a matter of unfinished business—a trivial obligation. Let me see?" and he flipped over several leaves of the memorandum book. "Ah, yes, this is it: 'Acceptance, one hundred and fifty.' No, that is not it. 'Note at bank'—wrong again. Here we have it: 'I. O. U., one dollar.' I had forgotten the amount," and he handed Frank a bill for that amount.

"Many thanks, Mr. Durham. Adversity is the common lot, and such cheerful assistance as that which you accorded me at New York City is of the kind that keeps the human heart warm with those who honorably expect to pay their debts. Now then, sir, to the important business mission which brought me here."

Vincent looked darkly suspicious, Frank mildly inquisitive, Randy wondered what was coming, and Pep was curiously expectant.

"The inauguration of two new photo playhouses at Seaside Park has offered a certain scope of opportunity for my line of specialization," proceeded Booth. "I have canvassed the town and have done some very satisfactory initial business, believe me, Mr. Durham."

"I am very glad to hear that," spoke Frank, heartily.

"Beyond my expectations, I may say," declared the enterprising advance agent. "You are open for curtain features, sir?"

"Of the right kind, most certainly," assented Frank.

"High class with me, sir, always," declared Booth. "I have one contract of quite some magnitude. It is a continuous one, with a feature that will enhance your business materially. Perhaps I had better show you. How is that, sir?"

The advance agent presented a card. Upon it a photograph had been pasted and under this was the reading:

"Who am I? Meet me face to face!"

"Why," smiled Frank in some mystification, "this is a picture of the back of a man's head?"

"Exactly so—that's just it!" nodded Booth, animatedly. "In me you see the inventor of that most original idea. I wish you to have that made into a slide. You throw the picture on the screen during the intermissions. A blank card is given to every person with the admission ticket. It is announced that the picture represents a well known local merchant. Who is he? The audience is given a chance to vote and the cards are collected. To those who guess correctly a one-pound box of finest chocolates is delivered next day. These confections, done up in handsome boxes, you pile up in your front windows with a neat placard explaining the scheme. A custom drawer; eh, Mr. Durham?"

"Why, I must say it is quite a novel and ingenious plan," admitted Frank.

"Got to have some attraction like that to interest new business, sir," declared Booth. "I have presented the plan to you first, because you stood my friend in time of need and because I am informed that you operate the leading playhouse here at Seaside Park."

"Are you authorized to make a deal on that business, Booth?" inquired Vincent, in a blunt, matter-of-fact way.

"I am," replied the advance agent with emphasis. "My client will sign a contract. He is one of the most reliable business men in the community. In later curtain features, first the rear view and then the front view and advertisement of my client's business will be delineated on the screen. I have several other features to follow this one. I can make it worth your while to enter into a contract."

"I see no objection to your proposition," returned Frank, after a moment's reflection. "I dislike any prize lottery contests, or anything that approaches the gambling idea; but this suggestion of yours seems clean and honest."

He went over details with Booth and was pleased to realize that quite a neat little income was promised from this unexpected feature of the entertainments.

"I declare, that is the first coherent scheme I ever knew Booth to put through," asserted Vincent, as the advance agent took his departure. "If he sticks at this in a business-like way it looks as if he would make some real money. He goes off on a tangent every once in a while, Durham. You needn't be surprised if he drops in some day with one of his wild schemes, like dropping free tickets over the town from a balloon."

"Ready to go to the bank, Randy?" inquired Frank, in quite a flutter, taking the bank book from a pigeonhole in the desk.

"Yes," replied Randy, taking a neatly done-up package from his tin cash box. "I've sorted out everything above fifty cents for deposit."

"That's right—always keep a good supply of small change on hand," advised Jolly. "I say, Durham, what about the daytime shows?"

"We had better canvass that situation during the day," replied Frank. "We might give it a trial, say, day after to-morrow."

"I don't think a morning show would pay us," suggested Vincent. "You might work in three matinees, though, especially when the beach gets more crowded."

Randy invited Pep to go down to the bank with him. They felt pretty good over the pleasant way things were going.

"We're in the swim, sure," declared Pep, animatedly.

"Yes, and drifting along most delightfully," agreed Randy.

"Sort of a howling capitalist; aren't you!" railed Pep, as they reached the bank, and with a due sense of importance his companion handed in bank book and money at the receiving teller's window.

"You needn't talk," retorted Randy—"you're 'a bloated bondholder'; aren't you?"

Pep winced at the allusion. As they passed down the steps of the bank they came face to face with two of their business rivals. They were Peter Carrington and Greg Grayson. Pep carelessly and Randy rather distantly bowed to the two boys and were about to pass on their way.

"Hold on," sang out Peter, in his usual abrupt style. "Had quite a house last night; didn't you? So did we."

"I heard so," observed Pep. "What's the matter with your private box department, though?"

"Oh, accidents will happen," returned Peter. "Say, look out for a big hit, though, in a day or two."

"That so?" said Pep.

"You bet! Isn't that so, Greg?"

Greg Grayson assented with a nod. He looked mean and probably felt the same way. He had sense enough to realize that his past record with the moving picture chums, taken in conjunction with his present appearance on a new scene, showed him up in a poor light.

"Yes, sir," vaunted Peter, swelling as if some big idea had sprouted in that dull brain of his; "we're going to spring a motion picture sensation on Seaside Park that will about make us."

"That's good," applauded Randy. "You deserve it if you have the right thing."

"Well, we just have," boasted Peter. "It's so good that I shouldn't wonder if it put everybody else in our line clean out of business."

"Meaning us, I suppose?" inquired Pep.

"Well, those who don't want to get hurt had better keep out of the way," advised Peter. "The National has come to stay, I can tell you that."

CHAPTER XVIII—THE GREAT FILM

"Durham, I feel that we've just go to get that film," spoke Ben Jolly.

He held in his hand a special letter from the National Film Exchange, and the lively piano player waved it about in a way that showed that he was unusually excited.

"Yes," nodded Hal Vincent, "this is one of those specials that come along only once or twice a year. The prize fights used to lead before people knew as much as they do now; but you take a royal coronation, or a national auto race, or an earthquake, or liner lost at sea, and that's the big feature that the public run after for about a month."

"You've got to get in at them at the start, though," suggested Jolly.

"Always. The event advertises itself and the film men give it a new start. Why, to open up for day shows, this flood film would be an attraction all of itself."

"Better keep up with the times," half laughed Randy. "You know how Peter Carrington is bragging about some new attraction that is going to put us out of business."

Frank and his chums were practically novices in the "movies" line. They, however, knew enough about the business to realize that the theme under discussion was one worth considering in all its bearings. Furthermore, they placed great reliance in the judgment of Jolly and Vincent. The letter they had received advised them that within two days the "Great Flood Series" of films would be offered for lease. The supply was limited and on this account one film had been apportioned to certain territory. The right to use the film, therefore, would go to the highest bidder in each district.

The flood film covered a national disaster in which a large section of the West had been inundated, causing immense loss to life and property. Public charity had been appealed to and there were relief funds all over the country. The interest in the event had not yet abated.

"It's a big feature," declared Ben Jolly. "My advice is to get it."

"And get it quick," added Vincent. "These attractions are grabbed for."

"But the cost?" suggested Frank.

"Oh, it is never ruinous," said Vincent. "See here, you can spare me best out of your most valuable staff. I'll go to the city and put the deal through, if you say so."

"What about those cornet solos, and the talking picture stunt, and the act you were going to put on the programme?" grumbled Pep.

"Oh, they will keep for a night or so," replied Vincent. "Another thing, I ordered my outfit, which was levied on at the stand down country where my last venture showed, sent to New York City before I knew I was coming down here. There's some new wardrobe properties I want, too, so I can do double duty while I am in the city."

It was decided that Vincent should go to New York and see what could be done about the flood film. The boys had figured up what price they could stand as a maximum figure, but considerable discretion was left to their representative. Randy and Pep strolled down to the depot with Vincent.

"See who's here," suddenly observed Randy.

Peter Carrington, in a loud, checked suit, alarming necktie and classy yachting cap, was at the depot with his two admiring cronies, Greg Grayson and Jack Beavers. He was talking in a loud, showy way, but as Beavers caught sight of Vincent he spoke quickly to Peter and they drew away from the spot. Peter entered the chair car when the train came in.

"Hello, going your way," observed Randy.

"Say, suppose he's after that new feature film?" inquired Pep, excitedly.

"Might be," observed Vincent, carelessly. "If that's the big card they were bragging about, they haven't landed it yet. Glad you mentioned that point, Pep. I'll get busy."

There was a great deal to attend to that day. The season had commenced with the finest of weather and it bade fair to continue indefinitely. Frank and Jolly spent several hours deciding on the matinee feature.

"Tell you what, fellows," he said to Randy and Pep, "Mr. Jolly thinks he had better take the week to get into our routine thoroughly. Mr. Booth was in to see us again this morning about some advertising he will put through at low cost. I hardly think we will try any day shows until next week, unless our competitors do. Then of course we will have to show our colors."

"Well, I can tell you that they are not asleep," declared Pep.

"How is that?" inquired Jolly.

"I saw my friend who works for them. He is building a big transparency to put across the front of the National. He don't know exactly what it is going to advertise, but he thinks a big film feature."

"The flood special, I'll bet!" guessed Randy at once.

"Aren't they a little premature?" advanced Jolly.

"We'll know to-night," said Frank. "Mr. Vincent will probably be back on a late train."

The boys were brisk and ready for the evening's entertainment when the hour arrived. There was every indication of a big attendance. What pleased Frank most was to notice that those who were waiting for the doors to open were mostly family people—children and residents. This spoke well for the reputation the Wonderland had already gained.

The first house was only fair. There was, however, a big gain at eight o'clock. Randy looked up from the ticket reel as a familiar voice struck his ear with the monotonous:

"Two tickets, please."

"No, no," he laughed, moving back the bill which Miss Porter presented, and bowing with deference to her companion, the portly Mrs. Carrington. "You must allow us the honor and pleasure of retaining you on the free list."

"Ridiculous, young man!" said the outspoken Mrs. Carrington, but she was forced ahead by the on-pressing crowd. Pep caught sight of them and hustled about actively securing two good seats among the few left.

Pep felt that he was on good behavior with the eyes of their lady patronesses upon them. When they arose to leave at the end of the hour he slipped over to the operator's booth and advised Frank of the presence of their distinguished company. The little party drew aside for a moment or two out of the path of the dispersing audience.

"We must certainly compliment you on your well ordered place, Mr. Durham," said Mrs. Carrington.

"And your tasteful selection of films," added Miss Porter, brightly. "As to your pianist, he is an expert, and your usher system perfect."

"Oh, pshaw! you are making fun of me," declared Pep, reddening.

"Oh, dear!" observed Mrs. Carrington with a sigh, "of course I am deeply anxious for the success of that headstrong nephew of mine. Now he has got into the motion picture business I can't quite abandon him; but I must say the National is crude and inartistic compared with your place here."

"Peter has our best wishes, Mrs. Carrington," declared Frank. "I can assure you of that. Of course we are business rivals, but it will be with entire fairness on our part."

"I am sure it will. I told you so, Mrs. Carrington," spoke Miss Porter. "Peter talks as though you were sanguinary enemies, but I knew it was nonsense as far as you are concerned. I don't like the man he has taken in with him, a Mr. Beavers, however. I told him so yesterday, but met with a rebuff for the interest I displayed in Peter's welfare."

"That little lady is our champion, all right," declared Pep, returning from escorting the ladies to their automobile.

When the boys came to reckon up the proceeds of the evening they found them to be several dollars over what they had taken in the first night. They were congratulating themselves on their continued good fortune when Hal Vincent put in an appearance. He had a great paper roll under his arm and looked brisk and contented.

"Well, Hal?" hailed Jolly, in a cheery, expectant way.

"I want to show you something," was the ventriloquist's reply as he opened the roll upon the table.

It contained six different four-sheet posters. They were high colored, well executed and attractive. They depicted striking and thrilling events of "The Great Flood."

"Twenty-five sets go with the films," he explained.

"And you've got the films?" said Jolly.

"I couldn't bear to leave them behind," replied Vincent, with a smile. "I've got them and the price won't break us—but it's at the cost of making a deadly enemy."

CHAPTER XIX—GETTING ALONG

"Who's the enemy, Mr. Vincent?" inquired Frank, quickly.

"Peter Carrington."

"Pooh!" derided Randy.

"That doesn't sound so dangerous," declared Pep, lightly.

"Tell us about it, Hal," urged Jolly.

"There isn't a lot to tell," replied Vincent. "Pep here was right about Carrington being bound on the same mission to the city as myself. I found him at the National Film Exchange in great fettle. He had just closed a deal for the flood film."

"Then—then——" began Pep, in alarm.

"In his usual conspicuous and important way he had his check book out, fountain pen in hand, and ended up a grand flourish to his signature with a sort of triumphant grin at me as I entered the office.

"'Too late, Mr. Man!' he chuckled. 'Thought maybe you would be after the king attraction of the season, so I hot-footed it here from the train. There you are, sir,' and he handed the check to the cashier of the Exchange. 'Just pack up that film and the posters. Building a big transparency advertising it. If I can catch an early train we'll put it on to-night.'

"'I cannot deliver the goods on this check, Mr. Carrington,' said the cashier, politely but firmly.

"'I'd like to know why you can't!' flared up Peter. 'That check is good as gold, and my aunt has a little fortune in that same bank.'

"'All right, get someone in New York to indorse it and you can have the goods,' advised the cashier. 'It's no discrimination, Mr. Carrington. We make this a stringent rule with all out-of-town customers.'

"'Why, if you doubt my word, telegraph the bank at Seaside Park,' flustered Peter. 'Say, I'll do it myself. I'll have the cash wired on, but I shall enter a protest and a complaint with your superiors.'

"'That's all right,' smiled the cashier indifferently. 'I'll give you an hour to get the cash here. Only, remember we are likely to have other bids.'

"'I am on hand to take a look at the proposition,' I remarked just there. Peter nearly had a fit. Then he dived for the door. I found out that his figure was ninety-eight dollars for the week. I added two dollars. 'Wait the hour,' said the cashier.

"The hour was up and fifteen minutes over the limit when Peter rushed upon the scene once more," narrated Vincent. "He pulled a big wad of bank notes out of his pocket. 'Pack up that film,' he ordered sourly, 'and cancel all our other orders. I'm going to a new place where they won't question my credit on a measly sum like ninety-eight dollars.'

"'The film is sold for Seaside Park,' explained the cashier. 'The Wonderland has overbid you. You are overdue.'

"'Hold on,' I put in, 'I don't want to take advantage of a competitor. Fair and square, Carrington. If you want the film, bid for it.'

"'Of course I'll bid for it,' boasted Peter. 'I'll give a hundred and five.'

"'And ten,' I said quietly.

"'Fifteen.'

"'And twenty,' I added.

"'Sho!' said Peter, flipping over the bills in his hand. I haven't much more ready cash here with me.'

"'I'll loan you on your check,' I told him and the bluff took. I had only the hundred and fifty you gave me, but I was nervy, and it beat Peter. I fancy Jack Beavers had set a limit, or the real money wasn't flush at the National; anyhow with a snarl and a scowl Peter gritted his teeth at both of us and decamped."

Late as the hour was the motion picture chums were so interested in the new film that they had to give it a trial run. It was all the lurid advertising claimed for it from start to finish, and it took thirty-five minutes to run it— the scenes depicted held the interest.

"It's well worth the money," declared Ben Jolly enthusiastically. "Now then, to exploit it to the limit."

The transparency frame built for the National remained in place, but its muslin covering did not contain the announcement expected by Peter and his satellites. Even Hal Vincent, well as he knew Jack Beavers, was greatly surprised when he was told the next day that the space was devoted to booming a recent sparring match.

"It's pretty bad taste," he criticised. "It will take with a certain element, but it won't help in getting the good people and the stayers."

The flood film was widely advertised and put on that Thursday night. The posters made a fine show in the various store windows of the town. A private school came en masse to the first evening entertainment. A ladies' charitable association, active in raising a fund for the flood sufferers, was among the audience Friday night.

"It's a go," voted Ben Jolly, as Randy reported over a hundred people turned away from the doors. "If I were you, Durham, I would wire the Exchange for a thirty days' contract on that film."

This was done. A big house was expected for Saturday night and it had been decided to run two matinees from three to five beginning Monday. This crowded a little but not to any noticeable discomfort.

Pep, always on the scent for information regarding their competitors, came in with a new bulletin at supper time.

"Things are getting sort of mixed down at the National, I hear," he remarked.

"How's that, Pep?" questioned Jolly.

"They had a rough crowd among the audience last night and there was a fight. Two women fainted and several had their pockets picked by some fellows from that new Midway they started last week outside of the concession belt."

"I noticed Jack Beavers with a couple of hard-looking fellows yesterday afternoon down at the Midway," said Vincent. "That won't pay them, I can tell you."

"If the rough crowd have begun their work at the National we may expect them to make the rounds," said Jolly. "Keep a sharp eye out, Pep."

"I'll do just that," was the prompt response.

As anticipated by the motion picture chums and their friends, the throngs that evening beat all records. Pep forgot to look for suspicious characters or trouble. Everything went smoothly up to the last show, when he noticed four swaggering fellows come in. They crowded their way to the front and made a noisy shuffling with their feet and talked loudly. A few minutes later a like group gained admittance and took seats among the rear rows of seats. There were cat calls and signals between the two groups and Pep scented trouble.

Vincent, who until he went on the programme the next week helped Pep to keep things in order, came up to his young friend just as the first film of the third series was being run off.

"I say, Pep," he observed, "two of the fellows in that quartette in front there are the same fellows I saw with Jack Beavers. They look ripe for a demonstration."

"You mean they may have been sent here to make trouble for us?"

"And rush the crowd in the hope of picking a few pockets—that is their general programme, yes."

"I wish we could get one of the beach policemen to show himself," said Pep. "That would scare them off. Those officers are friendly to us, but won't make a move until a real row is on."

"I think I can help out on this proposition," remarked Vincent, and Pep noticed that he passed through the doorway leading to the living apartment, behind the main room.

When the lights came on for a moment between the first and second film Pep stared in blank surprise at a figure standing against the side wall. It was that of a police officer fully uniformed, even to the stout club usually carried. He was not ten feet away from the quartette that had made Pep so apprehensive.

"It's Mr. Vincent," guessed Pep—"good for him!"

The versatile ventriloquist it was. His extensive wardrobe had provided a disguise that cooled down the four unwelcome visitors from the start. Vincent stood like a statue where he had posted himself, as if on duty. When the lights went off he drew even nearer to the quartette, and they seemed to accept the fact that he was there for their benefit and that it would pay them to behave themselves.

Vincent was a good deal surprised when someone came close to him down the aisle next to the outer wall of the building. He was almost startled when the words were whispered in his ear:

"Officer, I want you to help me as soon as this film is over."

"In what way?" inquired Vincent.

"The two men at the end of the front seats here—Midway crowd—I want them."

"Want them?"

"Yes, I am an officer from the city—I'll show you my credentials later. The two fellows I mention have led me a long hunt—it's a burglary case."

"What do you want me to do?" inquired Vincent.

"They will show fight, both of them, the minute their eyes light on me. You grab the second fellow. I'll attend to the other one. Then send the usher out for more police help."

"All right," assented Vincent, "only do all this quietly as you can. We don't want to hurt the reputation of the show by any rough work."

"Oh, they'll wilt when they see they're cornered. Another word-whisper."

"Yes?"

"Help me to do this job neatly and there's a fine reward to divide."

CHAPTER XX—A RICH FIND

As the lights came on again the man who had spoken to Vincent moved forward so as to intercept the two end men on the second row of seats. One of them, who had arisen the moment he fixed his eyes on the officer from the city, sat down quickly. He pulled his next companion by the sleeve, who slunk down with him.

All this Vincent noticed, and Pep, guessing that these actions meant something, glided to the side of the ventriloquist.

"What is it, Mr. Vincent?" he inquired breathlessly.

"I hardly know myself yet," said Vincent.

"I want you, my man!" spoke the city officer just here.

He reached out and grabbed the slinking man by the collar.

"That one also," was added sharply, and Hal Vincent pounced upon the other man in true official style. Pep heard what he took for signal whistles from the other members of the party, whom he noticed burrowing their way through the crowd as if fearing detection themselves and anxious to get out of the way as fast as they could.

"Go out and tell a couple of beach officers we need them, Pep," spoke Vincent quickly. "This way," he added to the New York officer, and led his prisoner into the living rooms.

Pep hurried on his mission and returned with the officers sent for. He advised Frank and Randy that "something was up" and made sure that the latter got started for the rear with his cash box. Then Pep closed and locked the front doors securely.

He stood there on guard until the two policemen and the officer from the city came out with their prisoners. They had handcuffed them together and the captives looked sullen but subdued.

"I won't forget you," spoke the officer from the city as Pep let the little group get out into the street.

"Oh, that's all right," replied Vincent. "We're glad to have got through with the fellows without any row or publicity."

"What have those men been doing, Mr. Vincent?" inquired Pep as the doors were again secured and they went back into the living rooms.

"Some big burglary in New York, the officer said," explained the ventriloquist. "It seems he has been on their trail for a week. Located them at the Midway and traced them here to-night."

"Get your broom, Randy," ordered Pep, consulting his watch.

"What for?"

"We've got just forty-eight minutes before twelve o'clock. We want to sweep out by then. To-morrow's Sunday, when we won't do it, and the next day is Monday when we can't do it with the hustle and bustle of a double programme and two matinees. Besides, it's a satisfaction to see it all neat and in order over to-morrow."

"That's so," assented Randy, but he yawned, for it had been an arduous day for all hands.

The boys pitched in with ardor, Pep taking one side, Randy the other. There was more sand than dust, for the floor had been cleanly swept only that morning. There was, however, the usual lot of candy and popcorn boxes, torn programmes, and the general litter of the entertainment.

"You beat me, Randy," said Pep, as his companion rounded into the end of the center aisle near the entrance first with his heap of swept-up rubbish.

"I'll get the box and the dust pan," volunteered Randy, "and we'll soon have the rubbish out of the way."

While his comrade was gone for the utensils in question Pep began poking about in the accumulated heap swept up. He always did this before the heap was placed in the rubbish box and dumped out of a side window into a coal box standing beneath it. Very often they found little articles of value—once a pair of ladies' gloves, a baby's hat twice, rings, and after nearly every performance pennies, nickels, and once a dollar bill. A list of these articles of any value was made and placarded on a neat card labelled "Owner Apply," tacked up on the ticket seller's booth outside.

"A plugged nickel and two suspender buttons," laughed Pep as a result of his explorations as Randy reappeared.

"I kicked something!" announced Randy, and sure enough something that rattled skidded across the floor from the edge of the dust heap.

"Why," replied Pep, picking up the article in question, "it's a chamois bag."

"Something in it?" questioned Randy.

"Think so? I'll see," and Pep probed. "I say," he added with animation, "look here, Randy!"

Both boys viewed in amazement the object Pep had extracted from the little chamois bag. It sparkled and dazzled.

"Gold!" uttered Randy.

"And diamonds!" added Pep with zest. "It's a necklace. It's handsome enough to be real, but that can't be."

"Why not?" challenged Randy.

"Oh, it would be worth a small fortune. Who's going to drop a thing like that in a ten-cent motion picture show?"

"We'll ask Mr. Vincent," suggested Randy, and Pep slipped their singular find into his pocket. They cleaned up the dust heap, set the rows of chairs in apple pie order and joined the others in the living rooms.

"I want to show you something, Mr. Vincent," said Pep, approaching the ventriloquist, who with Jolly was dispatching supper at the table.

"Why," exclaimed Vincent, as Pep handed him the chamois bag and he held up to the light the necklace it contained, "where in the world did you get this?"

"I should say so!" cried Jolly, his eyes fixed upon the shimmering article of jewelry.

"Randy swept it up," explained Pep.

"Is it good for anything?" inquired Randy.

"Is it!" projected Vincent forcibly. "I should rather say so! Those are genuine diamonds, and the other settings are valuable, too. Not less than a thousand dollars, and maybe five."

Pep gave utterance to an excited whistle. Randy looked bewildered. Frank, busy at his desk going over the contents of the cash box, arose from his chair and like the others became an interested member of the group.

"Some lady must have carried it with her and it dropped from her pocket," he suggested. "It is too late to-night to think of seeking an owner for it."

"Whoever it belongs to will be around looking for it quick enough," declared Vincent.

"I hope there will be some kind of a reward," said Randy.

"If there is, you get it," observed Pep.

"No, we divide," insisted his loyal chum.

"Well, wait till the reward is offered, will you?" laughed Jolly. "I say, Durham, our friend Booth must know of this. He'll get us a whole column in the newspapers. 'Exclusive and fashionable audience at the Wonderland. Sensational loss of priceless gems! Found by the proprietors. Consumed with anxiety to locate the owner. Latter appears—prominent society leader. Jewels restored and the Wonderland still running to crowded houses. See the great flood feature films!' Why, it's as good as the usual lost jewels for the actress."

Frank took charge of the chamois bag and deposited it in the tin cash box. This he locked up and as usual took it into one of the apartments where he slept.

"We shall have to keep special watch over all that valuable stuff until the bank opens Monday morning," he explained.

Randy hung around, wrought up with excitement over their wonderful find and anxious to talk about it. Pep was very tired and went to his cot to rest. Frank, Jolly and Vincent sat with their feet on the sill of an open window, enjoying the cool breeze from the ocean and indulging in pleasant comments on the first successful week of the Wonderland.

"With the flood film and the specialty act of the great family entertainer, 'Signor Halloway Vincenzo,' I predict we will capture the town next week," declared Ben Jolly.

"Guess I'll turn in, too," remarked Randy, after wandering about the room aimlessly for some time.

"All right, just turn out the light, will you?" asked Frank. "It's sort of nice to sit here with the moonlight streaming in."

Randy took off his coat and shoes and started for the apartment where Pep was fast asleep. It contained two cots. He had started over to give Pep a shake and make him get up and undress, when he chanced to pass one of the windows and glanced out.

"Fire!" he instantly shouted, and rushed out into the room where the others were.

"What's that?" challenged Frank, springing to his feet.

"Yes, right across the block," declared Randy. "You can see it from the side window. Look at that!"

A glare suddenly illuminated the room. Ben Jolly moved to the window and uttered a sharp whistle of surprise. Frank ran into his room and came out with his cap on. Then there was a rush for the little back stairs running into the yard behind the building.

"Wait for me!" called out Randy, struggling to put on his shoes.

"Hey! what's all the row?" hailed Pep sleepily, as Randy stamped his foot into a shoe, grabbed up his cap and coat and made a dive for the yard.

"Fire!" bawled back Randy. "Right near us, too! Hurry up!"

Pep sat up on his cot rubbing his eyes. Then a spurting glare from the fire lit up the room. He jumped to his feet and hurried out into the large room.

"It is a fire, sure enough," he exclaimed, glancing from the window. "It's that big building where they rent rooms to transients. The whole roof is ablaze and——"

Pep came to a sudden halt. Just stepping over the threshold of the doorway at the head of the yard steps, he was confronted by two men running up them.

One of them threw out one hand. It landed on Pep's breast, almost pushing him off his footing, and was accompanied by the gruff voice:

"Hey, you get back in there!"

CHAPTER XXI—THE TIN BOX

Pep was a quick thinker. He could not tell how it was, but the minute his eyes lighted on the two strangers he somehow associated them with the group from whom he had anticipated trouble earlier in the night. In fact he was not sure that they were not two members of the quartette who had been the object of the visit of the officer from the city.

"What do you want?" Pep instantly challenged.

For answer his assailant leaped forward and made a grab for him. Pep knew that the intrusion of these men could have no good motive. He dodged, seized a frying pan from the gas stove, and brandished it vigorously.

"I'll strike!" he shouted. "Don't you try to hold me!"

"Quiet the young spitfire," growled the second of the men, and although Pep got in one or two hard knocks with his impromptu weapon, he was finally held tightly by the arms from behind by one of the men. Pep let out a ringing yell, hoping to attract attention from outside, but his friends were by this time in the turmoil of the fire, and the few crossing vacant spaces were shouting and excited like himself.

"I supposed they had all rushed out to the fire," spoke the man who had first appeared. "Keep this one quiet, if you have to choke him."

Pep's captor threw him to the floor and pinned him there with his knee on his breast, despite his wrigglings. He managed to apply a gag. Then he rudely jerked Pep to his feet, holding his wrists together in a vise-like grip.

The flare from the fire and the bright moonlight illumined the room as clearly as day. Some vivid thoughts ran riot in the active mind of Pep as the other man went into one of the partitioned sleeping places.

"That's right," called out Pep's captor. "The boy who had the tin box carried it in there somewhere."

"Got it!" sounded in a triumphant tone two minutes later, and there was a rattle and a rustling sound.

Pep groaned inwardly. He could figure things out clearly now, he fancied. The intruders were the two former companions of those arrested not two hours before by the city officer.

"Then it was the fellow he was after that left the chamois bag," theorized Pep rapidly. "He didn't want it found on him, and he got word to these friends of his. They probably saw us looking at the necklace through the windows and planned to get it back. When Frank and the others ran out to the fire they hurried in here, and——"

"Got it; eh?" inquired Pep's captor, as his comrade reappeared.

"I have," chuckled the other, and busied himself rolling a pillow slip about the tin box. "Found it under a cot in there. Now then, quick is the word."

The man who held Pep gave him a sudden fling. Pep landed against the wall on the other side of the room with stunning force. The two men, hurriedly departing, directed a quick glance at him.

"That settles him," observed the foremost of the two, running down the outside stairs.

Pep was dazed for a moment. He actually fell back half stunned. His head had received a terrific bump. The instant a thought of the loss of their little treasure box drifted into his mind, however, he was on his feet in a flash.

He tore the obstructing handkerchief from his mouth and made for the open door, capless and out of breath. Pep darted down the stairs, his eyes glancing in every direction. The whole top of the building, three hundred feet away, was blazing now. There was a vacant space behind the Wonderland, and across this people were running in the direction of the fire. Pep could not make out his friends anywhere about. As his glance swept in the opposite direction he saw two shadowy forms headed on a run for the side street.

"It's them; I see them!" cried Pep, and he sprinted ahead, his eyes fixed upon the scurrying figures. They disappeared between two buildings. Then they came out on the street next to the boardwalk.

All along Pep's idea had been to get near enough to them to call upon others to assist him in detaining them as thieves. There was no police officer in sight, however, and people about were thinking only of getting to the scene of the fire. Then, as Pep came out upon the street into which the two men had turned, he saw them standing by an automobile. One of them was cranking it. The other had climbed into the rear seat.

"Stop those men! they have robbed us!" shouted Pep, putting for the spot where the automobile stood and addressing three or four persons who were hastening in the direction of the fire.

One of these halted and looked at Pep as if to take heed of his announcement, but his fellows urged him to come on and laughed at Pep. The outcry had hastened the movements of the thieves. The man in front of the machine jumped into the chauffeur's seat and seized the wheel.

"You shan't get away with our property!" declared Pep, gaining on the auto just starting up. "Help! Thieves! Police! Police!"

The man in the rear seat had placed the box by his side. He had both hands free. As Pep leaped to the step and clung there, he reached out both arms. He was a fellow of powerful build, and he was annoyed and angry at the pertinacity of their pursuer. Pep dodged his head and body aside, but the man got a hold on his coat and pulled him clear over into the machine.

"Now go on," he directed his companion. "I'll squelch the young wildcat."

"You won't! Help! Police—pol——"

The man had Pep down between his knees. He was cruelly brutal, squeezing him down out of view from the street and choking him into silence. Pep gave up all hope now. He was silenced and helpless. The machine made several turns to baffle pursuit, if anyone should follow, and started down a winding road leading into the country.

"Now you sit still there and keep your tongue quiet or I'll do worse for you next time," growled his captor, lifting Pep to the seat and holding to one arm.

"Why don't you pitch him out?" demanded the man acting as chauffeur. "We're past the hue and cry now."

"Not from a fellow with his sharp wits," retorted the other. "He'd find the first telephone, double-quick. He's made us a lot of trouble. I'll give him a long walk home for his meddling."

They were going at such a furious rate Pep knew that even if they passed anyone his shout would be incoherent and borne away on the wind. At any rate they were secure from pursuit except by an automobile like their own.

He foresaw the fate of the little tin box—carried away with its precious contents by these criminals, himself abandoned in some lonely spot to find his way back home as best he might. A desperate resolve came into Pep's mind, as glancing ahead he caught the glint of water. At the end of a steep incline a bridge spanned a small river. Pep got his free hand ready. Just as the front wheels of the machine struck the first timbers of the bridge, his hand shot out for the tin box in its pillow case covering, lying on the cushion between himself and his captor.

It was all done quick as a flash. A grab, a whirl, a splash, and the hurling object disappeared beneath the calm waters just beyond the outer bridge rail. The man beside Pep uttered a shout. He was so taken aback at the unexpected event that he relaxed his hold on his captive.

His cry had startled his companion at the wheel, who took it as a signal of warning of some sort, and he instantly shut down on speed. It was Pep's golden opportunity. Before the man beside him could prevent it, he made a nimble spring out of the machine, landed on the planking of the bridge approach, stumbled, fell, and then, as a crash sounded, dived into a nest of shrubbery lining the stream.

Pep did not wait to look back to trace the occasion of the crash. He heard confused shouts and knew that the two men had gotten into some trouble with the automobile. A light not over a hundred feet distant had attracted his attention. Pep darted forward. He ran into a barbed wire fence, then he crawled under it, and on its other side made out a farmhouse. The light came from the doorway of a big barn, where two persons, a man and a boy, were just unhitching a horse from a light wagon.

"Mister!" cried Pep breathlessly, running up to the men, "two thieves had wrecked their automobile right at the bridge. They have stolen a lot of money and jewelry. They tried to carry me away with them."

"Run for my gun, Jabez," ordered the farmer, roused at the sensational announcement. "Maybe they're the fellows who broke in here last week when we were away at a neighbor's."

The boy ran to the house. He soon reappeared with a clumsy double-barreled shotgun over his shoulder.

"Arm yourselves," directed the farmer, taking the weapon in one hand, the lantern in the other.

His son picked up a rake and handed a pitchfork to Pep. Then the boys followed the farmer as he strode towards the road.

The moonlight showed a wrecked automobile lying where it had been driven into a little clump of saplings—breaking them off two feet from the ground—and wedged in among the splintered branches. Evidently the amateur chauffeur had in his excitement made a turn at the wrong moment.

"Where's your robbers?" demanded the farmer.

"They saw us coming and have run away," declared Pep. "Mister, I want you to help me further and I will pay you for it."

"What doing?" inquired the man.

"As I told you, those men had stolen a lot of valuables. They were in a little tin box. Just as we were passing over the bridge here I saw my chance to outwit them. I flung the box into the river."

"What!" exclaimed the farmer.

"Sounds like a fairy story," remarked his son skeptically.

"You find some more help, so if those fellows show themselves we can beat them off or arrest them," observed Pep, "and I will prove what I have told you and pay you well for your trouble."

"Jabez, go and wake up the two hired men," directed his father.

"I'm a pretty good swimmer and diver," said Pep, after the boy had gone on his errand. "Is the water very deep?"

"Six or eight feet."

"Then the rake will help me," said Pep, proceeding to disrobe. He was stripped of his outer garments by the time the boy Jabez had returned with two sleepy-looking men. He was in the water at once. First he probed with the rake. Then he made a close estimate of the spot where the box was likely to have landed and took a dive.

Pep came to shore and rested for a few minutes. Then he resumed his labors. After a long time under water his head bobbed up. He uttered a shout of satisfaction and waved aloft the tin box, its dripping covering about it.

"All right," he hailed.

"A good deal in it, I suppose?" spoke the farmer, curiously regarding it.

"Yes, there is," replied Pep. "Hold it, please, mister, till I get my clothes on. I want you to take me to Seaside Park right away—two of you and the shotgun. If you'll do it you can charge your own price."

"That's fair," nodded the farmer.

He got the rig in the barn ready and told the two hired men they could go back to their beds. They seemed, however, to have roused from their sleepiness. Pep had told of a big fire in town, and that had influenced them to accompany the crowd, "just for the fun of the thing," as they expressed it.

Jabez drove, Pep holding the rescued box, the farmer between them with his shotgun ready for action. They saw nothing, however, of the robbers. The latter seemed to have decamped. If they were lurking in the vicinity, the sight of superior numbers kept them from making any demonstration.

As they got nearer to the town the glare of the distant fire was noted, and young Jabez whipped up the horse and made good time. The building on fire was pretty well consumed, but the fire department had saved adjoining structures. Pep directed Jabez to drive to the Wonderland by the rear route. He noticed that the living rooms were lighted up.

"Wait here for a minute," directed Pep to those in the wagon, dashing up the steps of the playhouse with his precious box.

CHAPTER XXII—A BIG REWARD

Pep burst in upon his friends filled to the brim with excitement. His impetuous nature anticipated a great welcome as he felt that he had done a big thing. As he crossed the threshold of the living room he found that his friends had apparently just returned from the scene of the fire.

Frank and Randy were at the sink washing the grime from their faces. As Pep learned later, they and Jolly and Vincent had been busy saving what goods they could from the burning building. Jolly was brushing the cinders from his coat with a whisk broom. Vincent was applying some court plaster to a burn on the back of his hand.

"There!" exclaimed Pep, planking the package down upon the table with a flourish. "It's been some trouble, but I got it."

"Hello, Pep," said Jolly. "Got what, may I ask?"

Pep felt rather hurt at the cool way in which his return was greeted. He did not realize that his friends were in ignorance of the burglarious event of the hour, and his own sensational experiences. He had just been missed and all hands supposed that he was lingering at the scene of the fire.

"Why, the box, of course," almost snapped Pep.

"What box?" questioned Randy.

Pep gave the wetted pillow case a jerk, freeing it of its enclosure, and the little cash box was disclosed.

"That box, of course," he announced. "What's the matter with you fellows? I guess you've been asleep while people have been stealing from you!"

Frank advanced to the table, curiosity dawning in his expression as he recognized the box.

"I don't quite understand," he remarked.

"Don't?" resented Pep. "Well, you ought to. Look at that," and he exhibited the bump on his head, received when one of the robbers had knocked him across the room and against the wall. "And that, too," and Pep held up his chin so the red marks on his throat showed. "Then, too," he continued, "half an hour ducking and diving in the cold waters of a creek at midnight is no grand fun, I can tell you!"

"Why, it looks as if our Pep has been up to something," observed Jolly, coming to the table.

"I've been down in front of the seat of an automobile and half choked to death," replied Pep tartly. "I say, Frank, it was a good thing that I didn't run off and leave the place unprotected, as you fellows did when that fire broke out. Open the box and see if everything is all right."

The appearance of the box and Pep's story made Frank and the others grasp that he was discussing something of importance not yet fully explained.

"You had better commence at the beginning all over again, Pep," Frank advised, "and let us know the whole story."

It did not take Pep long to recite his recent adventures. He had an interested audience. Frank drew the key of the tin box from his pocket when Pep had concluded his story. He applied it to the lock.

"Oh, the mischief!" fairly shouted Pep, glancing into it to find that all it contained was a collection of pennies, nickels and dimes. "I've been fooled, after all. These fellows rifled the box in some way——"

"Not at all," answered Frank, with a reassuring smile. "It is my turn to explain, Pep. When the fire broke out I thought instantly of the cash box and the treasure it contained, so I took out the bills and the necklace. Here they are," and Frank produced them from an inside pocket of his coat.

"Then—then——" stammered Pep, taken aback.

"Then you are just as much a hero as if you had saved a whole bank of money!" cried Frank, giving Pep a commending slap on the shoulder.

"It was a big thing you did, Pep," declared Randy enthusiastically.

Ben Jolly and Vincent added more approving words, and Pep warmed up to his usual self at the praise of his friends.

"There's the fellows outside to settle with," he suggested.

"Glad to do it," said Frank. "There must be at least thirty dollars in the box, so you have saved us a good deal, Pep."

"Didn't catch a weasel asleep when they came in here!" chuckled Jolly in Pep's ear. "You taught them something this time."

The farmer was very modest in his charges. "Two dollars covered the damages," he remarked, "and seeing the fire was worth half of that."

It was getting well on to morning by the time all hands were settled down. Vincent was the last to go to bed. He had got a card out of his pocket and said he had some business down town.

"It's to send a message to the city officer who took those two prisoners to New York on the last train," he explained to Frank. "Of course there is no doubt that the necklace was part of the proceeds of the burglary he arrested them for."

"I think you are right," agreed Frank.

A quiet day in reading and rest did wonders in refreshing the tired out motion picture friends after a week of unusual activity and excitement. All were up bright and early Monday morning.

"I tell you, this is genuine office business," said Frank, as he rested at noon from continuous labors at his desk.

"You take to it like a duck to water," declared Ben Jolly.

"Who wouldn't, with the able corps of assistants at my command?" challenged Frank. "Mr. Vincent took Mr. Booth off my hands. He knows the man much better than I do and, as he expresses it, understands how to keep that visionary individual in the traces. Pep and Randy seem to have just the ability to get our new programme into the very places we want them. Mr. Vincent has sifted out the supply men as they came along, and those letters you got off for me took a big load off my shoulders, Mr. Jolly."

"It all amounts to having a good machine and starting it right," insisted Jolly.

The boys felt a trifle anxious as it began to cloud up about one o'clock. A few drops of rain fell. It almost broke Pep's heart, Randy declared, to see people begin to scatter along the beach and made their way to shelters, and the hotels.

"I'll try and stem the tide," observed Vincent smartly, as a bright idea seemed to strike him.

He dived into one of the bedrooms and reappeared in his band costume, cornet in hand.

"Open the door, Pep," he directed. "Never mind routine this time—what we want to do is to get the crowd."

Vincent posted himself under the shelter of the canopy that ran over the ticket booth. Soon his instrument was in action. The delightful music halted more than one hurrying group. The inviting shelter beyond the open doors attracted attention. The word went down the beach. The shower would be over in an hour and here was a fine place to spend the interim.

"Twenty minutes to two and the house nearly full," reported Pep gleefully, to Jolly at the piano.

The shower was over in half an hour, but when the first crowd passed out there was another one ready to take its place. About half the seats were occupied when the second entertainment began, but during the programme as many more came in. The last matinee could not accommodate the crowd. The Wonderland caught the throngs going to the boats and trains as well as those arriving.

The boys and their friends were at supper when there was a visitor. He proved to be the officer from the city who had arrested the two burglars. He had come in response to the telegram Vincent had sent him. The latter told him about the finding of the necklace and added the story of Pep's later adventures.

"The necklace is down at the bank in our safety deposit box," explained Vincent. "We didn't want to risk having it around here any longer."

"I knew from the circumstances and your description that it is part of the plunder I am after," said the city officer. "I wish you would meet me at the hotel in the morning. I will have the local police head there. As a mere formality the goods will be delivered by you to him, who will turn them over to me. Then I will give you an order for your share of the reward."

Randy pricked up his ears and Pep looked interested.

"How much is it?" inquired Vincent.

"Five hundred dollars. I think it fair to divide it; don't you?"

"I know that will be very acceptable to our young friends here," assented Vincent, nodding at Pep and Randy. "All the credit for finding the necklace is theirs."

Pep and Randy were considerably fluttered. They had their heads together animatedly discussing their good fortune as Vincent accompanied his visitor to the door.

"I say, you lucky young fellows," hailed the ventriloquist airily, "what you going to do with all that money?"

"Oh, Randy and I have settled that," proclaimed Pep.

"Have, eh?"

"Yes, sir. That two hundred and fifty dollars goes into the capital fund of the Wonderland."

CHAPTER XXIII—THE BROKEN SIGN

"It blew big guns last night, fellows," observed Randy Powell.

"Yes, it has been working up to a storm for several days," said Ben Jolly, casting a weather eye through the open window in the living room.

Breakfast had just been announced by Jolly and as usual all were hustling about to put in an appearance for the famous home-cooked meal.

"We mustn't complain if we have a day or two of showery weather, Pep," spoke Frank.

"It means poor shows, though," lamented Randy.

"We can stand that," replied Frank. "I think we have been more than fortunate."

"I should say so," remarked Jolly—"six shows a day and the house a clear average of three-fourths filled."

"How are our friends down at the National doing, Pep?" inquired Vincent.

"Oh, so, so," was the careless reply. "They get their quota from the Midway crowd, which we don't want. My friend who works for them says they let things go half right, quarrel among themselves, and a few nights ago Peter Carrington had a crowd of his boy friends in a private box smoking cigarettes while the films were running. Peter doesn't speak to me now when we meet."

"I thought the building was coming down one time last night," spoke Jolly. "There was damage done somewhere, for I heard a terrific crash a little after midnight."

"There won't be many bathers to-day," said Vincent, glancing out at the breakers on the beach.

Pep finished his breakfast and went out to the front of the building to take a look at things. Just after he had opened the front doors his voice rang excitedly through the playhouse.

"Frank—Randy—all of you. Come here, quick!" Then as his friends trooped forward obedient to his call he burst out: "It's a blazing shame!"

"What is, Pep?" inquired Frank.

"Look for yourself."

"Oh, say! who did that?" shouted Randy.

He and the others stood staring in dismay at the walk, that was littered with glass, and then at the wreck of the electric sign overhead, which had cost them so much money and of which they had been so proud.

All that was left of it was "W—O—L—A—N—D" and woeful, indeed, the dilapidated sign looked. Broken bulbs and jagged ends of wires trailed over its face. Two bricks lay at the edge of the walk and the end of a third protruded from the bottom of the sign.

Randy was nearly crying. Frank looked pretty serious. Pep's eyes were flashing, but he maintained a grim silence as he went over to the edge of the walk and picked up one of the bricks.

"That was your 'great guns' you heard last night," observed Pep looking fighting mad. "Those bricks were thrown purposely to smash our sign. Why—and who by?"

There was not one in the group who could not have voiced a justifiable suspicion, yet all were silent.

"I think I know where that brick came from," proceeded Pep, trying to keep calm, but really boiling over with wrath. "I'm going to find out."

Pep tarried not to discuss or explain. The others stared after him as he marched down the boardwalk in his headstrong way. Pep had in mind a little heap of bricks he had seen two days before. They were made of terra cotta, red in color and one side glazed.

It was at the National that Pep came to a halt. Between the entrance and exit some attempt at ornamenting the old building had been made. There were two cement pillars and the space between them had been tiled. At one side was a plaster board and a few of the bricks that had not been used. The workman on the job had not yet tuckpointed the space he had covered, and had left behind some of his material, a trowel and other utilities.

Pep went over to the heap. He selected one of the bricks and matched it to the one he carried in his hand. He was standing thus when the door of the National opened and three persons came out. They were Peter Carrington, Greg Grayson and Jack Beavers.

"Hello!" flared up Peter, as he caught sight of Pep, "what are you snooping around here for?"

"I'm running down the persons who smashed our electric sign last night, and I'm fast getting to them," replied Pep. "Carrington, you're a pretty bad crowd, all of you, and I'm going to make you some trouble."

"What for? What about?" blustered Peter, and then he flushed up as Pep waved the brick before him.

"That brick and two others like it smashed our sign," he declared. "There probably isn't another lot of them in town except here."

"Well, what of it?" demanded Greg Grayson, sourly.

"I'm not talking to you," retorted Pep. "We did enough of that after your mean tricks at Fairlands. Whoever smashed our sign did it with some of your bricks. You needn't tell me they didn't start out with them from here. There's plenty of stones along the beach for the casual mischief maker. You're trying to break up our show. Soon as I get the proofs I'm after, I'll close yours and show you up to the public for the measly crowd you are."

"Say," flared up Peter, "this is our property and you get off of it, or——"

"Or you'll what?" cried Pep, throwing down the bricks and advancing doughtily.

"Easy, Carrington, easy," broke in Jack Beavers and he stepped between the belligerents, "Don't raise a row," he pleaded with Pep. "There's enough going on that's disagreeable without any more added." Then he followed Pep as the latter went back to the street. "See here, I don't want any trouble with you people," he went on in an anxious way. "So far as I'm concerned, I give you my word of honor I don't know the first thing about this sign business."

Pep looked at the speaker's face and was almost tempted to believe him.

"You needn't tell me!" he declared. "Those fellows are a mean lot and they ought to be punished."

Pep returned to the Wonderland with his tale. Frank tried to quiet him, but Pep's indignation had got the better of him.

"If you can make certain that the National crowd did this damage, we can make them pay for it," said Frank, "but I don't want to proceed on guesswork."

"Oh, you know as well as I do that they did it, Frank Durham!" stormed Pep.

"I think they did, yes," acknowledged Frank, "but if we go to making any charges we cannot prove Mrs. Carrington will hear of it, and I don't care to offend her. Drop it, Pep. We'll have to take our medicine this time. If it gets too flagrant, then we will go to the authorities with it."

Pep was not fully satisfied, however. He managed to see his friend who worked for the National a little later, and tried to enlist his coöperation in ferreting out the vandals who had damaged the electric sign.

The latter could not be replaced entire without sending to the city for some of the missing letters. This, however, led to one beneficial result. When the duplicate letters arrived some colored bulbs accompanied them, a suggestion of Jolly. Two nights later the brilliant sign invited and attracted attention in its new varicolored dress, showing up as the most conspicuous illumination on the boardwalk.

The gusty, showery weather got down to a chill unpleasant spell finally. On Thursday night the Wonderland was running, but to rather slim audiences. There were few venturesome visitors to the beach in the daytime and the matinee entertainments were curtailed.

That night, however, the Wonderland had never had a more enthusiastic audience. It was comprised of an entirely new crowd—people themselves in the entertainment business and general trade lines, who could pick only a slack business period to seek enjoyment. They knew what a good thing was when they saw it and their generous approbation of the flood film and of Hal Vincent's ventriloquial acts with his dummies made up for the lack of numbers.

"Fine thing!" said more than one.

When the second show began a good many who had gone out came back again. A pelting rain had set in, accompanied by a tearing wind. Randy had to keep the window of the ticket office closed as well as he could, and Pep shut the roof ventilators.

It was in the middle of the last film that a great gust of wind shook the building. In the midst of it the echo of the service bell of the life saving station down the beach reached the ears of the audience. Many began to get nervous. Just as the film closed there was a clatter and crash and pieces of the broken skylight in the roof of the playhouse clattered down.

There were cries and a general commotion. Many arose to their feet. The rain began to pour in from overhead.

CHAPTER XXIV—THE GREAT STORM

"We're going to have a night of it."

Ben Jolly spoke the words with a grim conviction that had its effect upon his friends. Each could realize for himself that they were face to face with an emergency.

When the skylight was partly shattered by a loose board blown across the surface of the roof, and the pieces of shattered glass and rain came beating down, the flood of illumination quieted what might have been a panic. Jolly had jumped to the piano stool.

"There is no danger," he shouted—"just a broken pane of glass of two."

Then he had resumed his seat and dashed off into a lively tune. People could see now that they were in no immediate peril and could easily get out. The dripping rain, however, dampered their amusement ardor. There was a movement for the exit and the last film was left unfinished.

Frank had got to Randy as soon as he could. He did not wish the report to get out that the Wonderland was in any way unsafe, or have anyone leave the place feeling that he had not got his full money's worth. He summoned Pep to his assistance after giving Randy a quick direction. The latter immediately proceeded to stamp the date and the seal of the Wonderland across some blank cards. Then he came out into the entrance archway with the others.

"Here you are!" shouted the lively Pep. "Everybody entitled to a free ticket. Good any night this week on account of to-night's storm. Let no guilty man escape!"

"Ha! ha! very good."

"This is liberal."

The crowd was put in rare good humor by Frank's happy thought. The doors were left open and those who did not wish to go out into the pelting storm, were told they were welcome to linger in the entrance and among the rear seats until the rain let up. Meantime, however, Jolly and Vincent were not idle. While their young friends were coaxing the audience into good humor, the former had found a ladder, of which there were several about the place. Vincent mounted it and got at the skylight.

It was pretty well broken and the wind threatened still further damage. Jolly remembered a large canvas tarpaulin in the cellar that had been used by the painters. By the time the front of the place was cleared of the people he and Vincent had the skylight well battened down and protected.

"We're going to have a bad night," he reported as he came down the ladder dripping. "A view of the beach from that roof to-night would make a great moving picture."

"I hope the storm won't move us, Mr. Jolly," said Frank a trifle uneasily, as a fierce blast shook the building.

There was nothing to do but to doubly secure all the doors and windows. The roof of the living room proved to be leaky, but the use of pans and kettles to catch the water provided against any real discomfort.

"I think we had all better stay up," suggested Jolly. "I was in one of these big coast storms a few years ago and before the night was through we had some work on hand, let me tell you."

The speaker proceeded to light the gas stove, put on some coffee to boil and then announced that he was going to make some sandwiches. This suited all hands. It seemed sort of cheery to nest down in comfort and safety while the big storm was blowing outside. Pep and Randy began a game of checkers. Vincent was mending one of his speaking dolls. Frank was busy at his desk. They made quite a happy family party, when all chorused the word:

"Hello!"

"Lights out," observed Jolly, himself the center of the only illumination in the room, proceeding from the gas stove.

"The electric current has gone off, that's sure," remarked Vincent. "That means trouble somewhere."

They waited a few minutes, but the electric lights did not come on.

"Light the gas, Randy" suggested Frank. "I think we had better light one or two jets in the playhouse, too, so we can see our way if any trouble comes along."

The playhouse was wired for electric lights, but had a gas connection as well. The jet in the living room was lighted.

Pep went out and set two jets going in the playhouse. They heard him utter a cry of dismay. Then he hailed briskly:

"Come out here. Something's happened."

They all rushed in from the living room. Something had, indeed, happened. Pep stood in half an inch of water, which was flowing in under the front doors.

"Why this rain must be a regular deluge!" cried Randy.

"It's not rain," sharply contradicted Pep.

"What is it, then?"

"Salt water. Hear that—see that!."

During a momentary hush they could hear a long boom as if a giant wave was pounding the beach. Then a great lot of water sluiced in under the doors.

"Open up, Pep," directed Frank, "we must see to this right away."

The moment the doors were opened a lot of water flowed in. But for the incline it would have swept clear over the floor of the playhouse. Meeting the rise in the seats, however, it flowed in about fifteen feet, soaking the matting and coming nearly to the boys' shoe tops. Then it receded and dripped away over the platform outside.

All along the beach the electric lights were out, but the incessant flashes of lightning lit the scene bright as day. Here and there among the stores lanterns were in use, even candles, and where they had gas it was in full play.

The beach clear up to the boardwalk was a seething pool now. Whenever a big swell came in it dashed over the walk and beat against the building lining it.

"See here," cried Randy in a great state of perturbation, "there isn't any danger of the boardwalk going; is there?"

"Part of it is gone already down near the slump," declared Frank. "Look, you can see the beach from here. I hope the waves won't upset any of the buildings."

"They can't, right here, Durham," declared Jolly promptly. "You see, there's a drop from us inland. The water will drain off, if it doesn't come in too heavy."

"I'll bet there's trouble over on the flats," suggested Randy. "See the lights moving around."

"Lock the doors, Pep," spoke Jolly. "We'll take a look around and see just how bad things are."

It was no easy task maintaining their footing on the boardwalk, for it was slippery and at places gave where it had been undermined. Once a big wave swept over the exploring party and threw them in a heap against a building. People came running past them from the lower level of the Midway.

They could hear the life saving corps yelling orders and the storm bell sounding out constantly in the distance. It was as they came to the street that cut down past the National, that Frank and his friends paused to survey a scene of great excitement.

The street, as has been already noted, dropped away from the boardwalk to a depression fully twenty feet below its level. This made it a natural outlet, not only for the waves that beat up over the boardwalk, but also for what drained laterally on both sides.

"Why, it's like a regular water course," declared Frank. "I say, there's someone needing help."

"Just look at the National!" exclaimed Pep, as they returned from carrying some crying children away from the menace of the flood.

The rival playhouse stood at the lowest part of the depression. A long platform ran to its entrance. This was fully four feet under water and the lower story of the place was two steps lower down. Here the surplus water had gathered, growing deeper every minute. The street in front was impassable, and running two ways a veritable river, which cut off the National as if it was an island.

"I hope no one is in it," said Frank.

"But there is!" cried Randy. "Look, Frank—that window at the side. Some one is clinging to the window frame."

The flashes of lightning, indeed showed a forlorn figure at the spot Randy indicated. And then Vincent, after staring hard, cut in with the sharp announcement:

"It's certainly Jack Beavers!"

"Hey, you!" yelled Pep, making a speaking trumpet of his hands and signaling Peter Carrington's partner. "Help me fellows," and Pep sprang upon a platform that had drifted away from its original place in front of some store.

Frank was beside him in a moment. Randy had got Jolly to help him tear loose a scantling from a step protection. He joined the others, using the board to push their unstable float along.

The water was over six feet deep and the scantling was not much help. A great gust of wind whirled them ten feet nearer to the playhouse building. At the same time it blew over the chimney on its top.

The boys saw the loosened bricks shower down past the clinging form in the window.

"He's hit!" shouted Pep. "He's gone down!"

Jack Beavers fell forward like a clod and disappeared under the swirling flood. In an instant the motion picture chums acted on a common impulse and leaped into the water after him.

CHAPTER XXV—CONCLUSION

It was a moment of great suspense for Ben Jolly and the ventriloquist as, without a moment's hesitation, the three motion picture chums dived from their frail raft. The surface of the flood was so strewn with pieces of floating wreckage—the bottom and sides of the newly formed water way so treacherous—that it was a tremendous risk to get into that swirling vortex.

Frank and his companions were no novices in the water. They saw that Jack Beavers had been struck down from the window sill by the falling bricks, and had probably been knocked senseless. Almost immediately after diving the heads of the boys appeared on the surface.

"Got him!" puffed Randy.

"Lift him up," directed Frank, swinging out one hand and catching at a protruding window sill of the building. This purchase gained, all exerted themselves to drag up the limp and sodden form of Peter Carrington's partner. Frank and Randy kept the upper part of the man's body out of the water. Pep swam after the floating platform they had used a a raft. Jack Beavers, apparently more dead than alive, was placed upon it. His rescuers pushed this over to where the water was shallow and then carried the man into a drug store fronting the boardwalk.

"I suppose I had better stay with him," observed Vincent, as Beavers, after some attention from a physician who happened to be in the drug store, showed signs of recovery. "I know him the best, although I can't say truthfully that I like him the best."

"Yes, he's struck hard lines, and it's a sort of duty to look after him," said Ben Jolly.

He and the boys put in nearly two hours helping this and that group in distress among the storekeepers of the slump. They got back to the Wonderland to find that its superior location had saved it from damage of any consequence.

A wild morning was ushered in with a chill northeaster. Daylight showed the beach covered with wrecked boats and habitations. The tents over on the Midway were nearly all down. The National was still flooded and the street in front of it impassable. Very few of the frame buildings, however, had been undermined.

The worst of the storm was over by afternoon, but no entertainment was given until the next evening. A big transparency announced a flood benefit, and five thousand dodgers telling about it were circulated over the town.

It was a gala night for the Wonderland. There were few of the minor beach shows as yet in condition to resume operations, and after twenty-four hours of storm everybody seemed out.

"At least seventy-five dollars for the benefit of the poor families down on the beach," observed Pep. "Say, let me run down and tell them. It will warm their hearts, just as it does mine."

"All right," acceded Frank. "I guess you can promise them that much, Pep."

Frank and Jolly stood in front of the playhouse talking over affairs in general as Pep darted away on his mission of charity. A well-dressed man whom Jolly had noticed in the audience, and one of the last to leave the place, had loitered around the entrance. Now he advanced towards them.

"Is there a young man named Smith connected with your show?" he inquired.

"Yes, sir," replied Frank. "He has gone on a brief errand, but will soon return."

"I'll wait for him," said the stranger, and he sat down on the side railing.

Frank went inside as Randy appeared with his cash box. Jolly remained where he was. Finally Pep came into view briskly, happy faced and excited.

"Some one to see you—that man over there," advised Jolly.

"Is that so? Stranger to me. Want to see me?" he went on, approaching the stranger.

"If you are Pepperill Smith."

"That's my name," vouchsafed Pep.

"The same young man who was the guest of Mr. Tyson at Brenton?"

"Guest!" retorted Pep, in high scorn. "Oh, yes, I was a guest! Fired me the first time he got mad."

"Oh, well, we all have spells of temper we are sorry for afterwards," declared the man smoothly.

"Is Mr. Tyson sorry?" challenged Pep.

"He is, for a fact. You see—well, he gave you some papers, cheap stocks or bonds; didn't he, instead of cash for your services? He thought maybe you'd rather have the money. I've got a one hundred dollar bill for you. If those papers are lying around loose you might hand them over to me."

"I haven't got them," said Pep, and the man looked disappointed. "Maybe my friend preserved them. Oh, Mr. Jolly," and Pep called the pianist over to them and explained the situation.

"H'm!" commented Jolly thoughtfully, when Pep had concluded his story, and glancing keenly at the stranger, "you seem to have discovered some value to the stock you refer to."

"Oh, I suppose these stock brokers know how to juggle them along," responded the stranger, with assumed lightness.

"Well, as I understand it, they were given to my friend Smith."

"Undoubtedly—why, yes, that is true."

"As their custodian," continued Jolly, "I want to look into this matter."

"I wouldn't. Waste of time. All a tangle," insisted the stranger. "Look here, let me give the boy two hundred dollars."

"You can give Pep all you want to," observed Jolly, "but I shall advise him to see how the market stands on that stock before he delivers those securities."

"Hum! ha! quite so," mumbled the stranger in a crestfallen way.

"And we will let Mr. Tyson know our decision in a day or two."

"I see—well, I will report the result of my negotiation to my client."

"Negotiation? Aha! Client? A lawyer, then," observed Jolly, as the man reluctantly moved away. "Pep Smith, I'll investigate that stock of yours with the first break of dawn. There's something more to this than appears on the surface."

"Wasn't that Jack Beavers I just saw you talking to?" inquired Hal Vincent of Frank, as the latter approached him on the boardwalk.

"Yes, poor fellow," replied Frank. "I have been having quite a conversation with him."

"Making a poor mouth about his misfortunes, I suppose?" intimated the ventriloquist.

"Not at all, Mr. Vincent," explained Frank soberly. "He is all broken up, but more with gratitude towards us for saving his life the night of the storm than anything else. He acts and talks like a new man. Peter Carrington and Greg Grayson left him in the lurch with a lot of debts, and he is trying to get on his feet again."

"In what way?"

"Some friend has happened along and is willing to fix things up at the National. He came to me to say that he felt he had no right to come into competition with us, after owing his very existence to our efforts the other night."

"What did you tell him, Durham?"

"I told him to go ahead and make a man of himself and a success of the show, and that he need expect nothing but honest business rivalry from us."

"Durham," spoke the ventriloquist with considerable feeling, "you're pure gold!"

The bustling pianist appeared on the scene all smiles and serenity at that moment.

"Where's Pep Smith?" he inquired.

"Up at the playhouse."

"That so? All right. Come along, and see me give him the surprise of his life. You know I went down to Brenton to see Mr. Tyson about that stock? Well, I'm back—minus the stock. I've got something better. Look there."

Ben Jolly held a certified check before the dazzled eyes of his friends. It read: "Pay to the order of Pepperill Smith Two Thousand Dollars."

"This good fortune will about turn Pep's head," declared Frank Durham.

"Why, those shrewd fellows will get double that out of it," said Jolly. "It seems that the company is on the rocks, but a reorganization is being attempted and it can't be put through without a majority of the stock. Pep's holdings fit in snugly, so they had to pay me my price."

Pep Smith gasped as Jolly recounted all this over again to him in the living room back of the photo playhouse.

"What are you going to do with all that money, Pep?" inquired Randy.

Pep waved the precious bit of paper gaily and jumped to his feet with glowing eyes.

"What am I going to do with it?" he cried. "And what could I do but put it into the Wonderland business fund! Why, just think of it! When the season is over at Seaside Park we have got to look for a new location; haven't we?"

"That's sure," agreed Ben Jolly. "You boys have made a success of the motion picture business so far and I want to see you keep it up."

And so, with both playhouses in the full tide of prosperity, we bid good-bye to our ambitious young friends, to meet again in another story to be called: "The Motion Picture Chums on Broadway; Or, The Mystery of the Missing Cash Box."

"My, but we have been lucky!" declared Randy.

"That's what," added Pep.

"Well, we've had to work for our success," came from Frank.

THE END

9 781836 573401